THE
TYRANT
FROM
ANOTHER
WORLD

DIEGO MILES

BOOK 1 OF TYRANNICAL

CONTENTS

Chapter 1

CLEAN SLATE

"Sir Overlord, you may fire when ready." A voice blared over the intercoms.

Sir Overlord, a title given to the supreme being of the universe and sole ruler of the Malfadian Empire. There was only one worthy of such a title—himself.

Ogenos stared through the glass walls of his throne room. The four pupilless baby-blue eyes of his reflection stared back.

He blinked slowly, gazing at the scenery before him: space. Dozens of little stars dotted the black canvas like sparkling specks of dust. There were many places to look, but his sights were fixated on a single target.

Within the void of space were three celestial objects. The biggest of them had a blue and green color scheme fit for a planet abundant with life. Orbiting the planet were two smaller spherical objects. One of which was red, covered with all sorts of craters and bright lights—a colonized moon.

The other spherical object was pitch black. Had it not been for the shimmering lights on its surface, it would've blended in perfectly with the blackness of space. However, the small lights on the surface weren't coming from sprawling cities like on the red moon. In fact, they were much brighter than the red moon's lights and illuminated the mechanical appearance of the black object, showing its exterior was divided into three sections. The top and bottom sections of the black object spun right, while the middle spun left.

It wasn't a moon, but rather a moon-sized ship—a colossus.

Unlike the red moon, which orbited the side of the planet, the black ship positioned itself above the planet.

For a long time, Ogenos said nothing. He just stared at the planet. *All those people... All those lives... What were they living for?* He contemplated briefly before raising one of his four arms.

In his three-fingered grasp was a green metallic triangular device covered in symbols. Ogenos trailed one of his long, jointed purple fingers over the symbols, and the whole device turned blue.

A moment after, a menacing red light glowed from the bottom of the colossus. The light grew brighter and brighter, almost becoming as blinding as the system's sun. Ogenos stared at it, unblinking.

Finally, the brightness dimmed, and a red stream of pure energy shot out from the ship's bottom directly into the planet below. The red energy, which could be seen from orbit, traveled across the entire globe within seconds.

The red beam lasted for a minute, then abruptly stopped.

A second later, the planet shifted and distorted, gradually cracking into fragments that spanned continents. Just as it was coming apart bit by bit, the whole thing imploded, releasing a large shockwave.

By then, the green and blue planet was no more. It had been broken into various chunks, and with its atmosphere blown away, it took on a molten appearance.

Just like that, all those trillions of lives were extinguished in a mere instant. The soldiers, the workers, the guilty, the innocent—all of them. Gone.

Ogenos wasn't remorseful. It needed to be done. Otherwise, that rebel group would've continued to defy his rule. Sure, he could've scoured the planet for their home base and eliminated the rebels without sacrificing a whole world, but that would be like searching for a needle in a haystack. In his experience, it's much easier to just incinerate the whole haystack.

Besides, there was still the red moon. With their capital gone, the survivors' only options were to bend the knee or experience a slow death. They'd make the right choice in due time.

With that resistance gone, there was no one left to oppose Ogenos, as they were the last surviving rebel group—which meant he had officially achieved total universal domination! This was a cause for celebration!

With his victory assured, the time for parties was now, especially since a new golden age would fall upon the Malfadian Empire pretty soon.

And yet, despite all of that, Ogenos felt... nothing.

Something about his victory felt hollow. How could it not? Those rebels weren't a challenge whatsoever. The Malfadian Empire had been fighting them for a little over a century, and the only reason their war even lasted that long was because Ogenos had given himself and his grand empire multiple handicaps.

It was fun for the first decade, but after a while, it became the same routine. Sure, he could've ended the war at any point and time. But, as boring as it was, it'd become the only thing he had to look forward to. It was quite literally the *only* highlight of his days for these past few decades.

And now it was over. As inevitable as it was, he finally won. But the victory felt so bland. There was no grand finale. No final clash or epic showdown. No last words from the enemy commander. It was just over after a single click of a button...

The anti-climatic nature of it all was... *infuriating.*

Instinctively, Ogenos clenched his fists, followed by a crackling shatter that echoed through the room. He looked at his hand, seeing the triangular device was nothing more than fine dust now.

Ogenos shook his head and turned back to the fractured planetoid. It drifted through the void of space, silently and aimlessly.

The weight of total victory was gradually settling onto him, and it was suffocating. He'd achieved everything he ever wanted, ever could want, and then some. Yet, his accomplishment felt so underwhelming. "What a shame. I became who I wanted to be," He grumbled, wiping the dust off from his hand.

Ogenos turned from the glass wall and strode over to his throne barefoot, walking up a long strip of white metallic stairs in the process. Each step he took rattled his purple ceremonial armor; as he walked, his purple and red-colored cape flapped behind him, despite there being no wind or ventilation in the room.

Upon reaching the top, he plopped his big self onto his throne. The throne was designed to have armrests for all four of his arms, though because of that, it was shaped weirdly. Despite its odd appearance, it was quite comfortable.

Ogenos had no chance to snuggle into his cold seat before the triangular door ahead of him glowed purple, then dissolved into pure energy.

Then, a figure waltzed in from the opening, joyously extending their arms. "Congratulations on total victory, Sir Overlord!" they announced cheerily. It was the same voice from the intercoms.

Ogenos recognized the figure as his second-in-command, the Supreme General. "Val." He clicked in response without eyeing him.

They were of the same species, possessing similar builds. Both had four arms, four pupilless eyes, three fingers and toes, a hardened exoskeleton, and a spider-like face.

That was where their similarities ended.

While Ogenos was on the more muscular side, Val possessed a slender physique and had a hot-pinkish exoskeleton, as opposed to Ogenos's purple exoskeleton. Val's eyes were also a deep dark purple, reminding Ogenos of their homeworld's violet sun.

Val stepped closer to the throne, tilting his head. "Is something wrong, Sir Overlord?" He questioned, perhaps sensing Ogenos's bothered aura.

Ogenos shifted in his throne, propping one of his hands up to rest his head on. "Now, why would you ask that?" He said sarcastically, still looking forward.

"It's just... you haven't looked at me in a few hours, Sir Overlord."

That was a true statement. Even now, Ogenos was looking at Val's purple hair and not Val himself.

In Ogenos's defense, Val's hair was pretty unique. It was already rare for a malfade to have hair. Ogenos himself was bald, but he often hid that fact with his four-horned helmet. The thing with Val's hair was that it flowed upward in a wavy motion, as if it was in a zero gravity environment. Plus, it was incredibly long—so long, in fact, that the end of it was at eye level with Ogenos, even though Val was at the foot of the stairs.

"Am I unsightly to you?" Val asked, sounding hurt.

Ogenos finally looked down at his second-in-command, sorely wishing he hadn't.

Val wore his pink-tinted armor with purple-colored elbow and knee pads. A purple cape flapped behind him like he was some sort of superhero. The worst part about Val's outfit was the diamond-plated collar wrapped around his neck.

You look awful. Is what Ogenos wanted to say, but he resigned himself to being polite and simply responded, "No."

His answer only made Val click his mandibles in confusion. "Then what appears to be troubling you? Say the word, and I'll have my top soldiers eradicate it this instant."

If only it were that simple. Ogenos sighed, then looked out into space.

His gaze was once again set on the fractured planet, believing those who once lived on that miserable rock had it easy. They got to live their life, find happiness, then die. Meanwhile, Ogenos was stuck in a perpetual cycle of unfulfillment and boredom. It got so bad that sometimes he wished his enemies won.

Val glanced between Ogenos and the fractured planet. He'd make a small, happy-sounding chirping noise. "Oh, I see."

"You see what," Ogenos asked blankly, still staring into space.

"I know what your problem is."

"You do?" Ogenos sat up in his seat, giving Val his full attention.

Val's four eyes curled in giddy excitement upon seeing Ogenos focus on him. "It's so very obvious, Sir Overlord. Your latest conquest has left you unsatisfied." Ogenos didn't think the source of his poor mood would be so easy to pinpoint. Then again, what else could it be? "Oh, but don't you worry. I suspected something like this would happen long ago, so I prepared something in advance." Val pulled something out from the hidden compartment of his leggings. "Behold. The solution to your problems."

He held the object up high, proudly presenting it to

Ogenos. It was a light blue orb covered with green triangular symbols. The symbols faded and reappeared gradually, always moving.

Ogenos was thrilled that this object would be the answer to his troubles, but he wasn't sure what he was looking at. "What is it?"

"I call it the transporter. This will be your key to new worlds!" The transporter hovered out of Val's hand and into Ogenos's.

He gripped the transporter softly. Its smooth surface was relaxing to the touch, but not relaxing enough to prevent a hint of anxiety from rising within. "Val... What do you think my problem is, exactly?"

"You're not content with the domination of this universe. You want to conquer more!" Ogenos's hopes were dashed as he realized Val didn't know what his problem was at all. "Admittedly, I had thought about this outcome for a long time, ever since the eradication of those hairless primates. With your undeniable power, I knew it was only a matter of time until all kneeled before you. So, I had Bellows do some research. His findings proved rather fruitful."

Ogenos slumped back in his seat, half disinterested and half wanting to see where this was going.

"It turns out those spiritual fanatics we destroyed two centuries ago were onto something. Other planes of existence *do* exist. The multiverse is real!" He pointed to the transporter. "And that device in your mighty hand will be the key to unlock the door to them all." Ogenos looked down at the transporter. "Think of all the planets you could destroy. The civilizations we could dominate. The slaves we could exploit!" Val declared excitedly, much more enthusiastic than Ogenos could ever hope to be. "We'd have access to limitless resources. The Malfadian Empire would be unstoppable, as it's always been!"

Ogenos thought about it, and for a moment, a spark of interest formed in his eyes.

Val had a point. New universes meant new worlds. New worlds meant unfamiliar places and people. Things he'd never seen and experienced would be available to him. He'd finally feel excitement again!

But, the more he thought about it, the less worthwhile it seemed.

Sure, he'd have access to fresh new experiences and unique, never-before-seen lands. And he might even meet his equal. But what then? What if he conquers all there is to conquer and sees all there is to see? What if he becomes...absolute?

The thought of dominating the multiverse felt no more satisfying than actually dominating his universe. The spark in his eyes soon died.

Val was quick to notice. "Something wrong, Sir Overlord?"

Ogenos grumbled. The Supreme General had always been observant and attentive to even the slightest shift of things. This was one of the few times Ogenos wished he wasn't.

I have to tell him something. He'll never shut up otherwise. He looked down at Val, who tilted his head in anticipation. "As tempting as it sounds to conquer other universes, this doesn't seem worthwhile."

"Huh?" Val's expression dropped. Not in sadness or disappointment, but pure confusion.

Ogenos immediately recognized the mistake he made. What kind of conqueror doesn't want to conquer? A bad one. "I doubt the other worlds will be as resilient as the ones here."

"Ah." Val clicked his mandibles intently. "I suppose that is a possibility."

Nice. Ogenos complimented himself for the swift recovery.

"Still, we'll never know until we breach the veil! Plus, it wouldn't hurt to expand the empire." Val countered.

Ogenos grunted, not having anything to argue against Val's point. Truthfully, he had no real reason not to invade other universes. He simply didn't want to. "But what if we don't?"

Val jolted at Ogenos's sudden comment. "Sir Overlord, are you, by chance, feeling unwell?"

One of Ogenos's free hands curled into a fist. Val's cluelessness agitated him, but he managed to hide his anger. "Now that we've dominated our universe, it just makes sense to look inward instead of outward."

"Sir Overlord, please. You're starting to sound less like a malfade and more like an inferior lifeform. You wouldn't want to live like them, would you?"

Ogenos's anger flared up. "What is that supposed to—" He paused, mentally repeating what Val had said several times. His anger disappeared as suddenly as it had appeared. "Wait, what did you just say?"

"I said you're starting to sound less like a malfade and more like an inferior lifeform." Val raised a pink jointed finger. "A God such as yourself deserves more than what those meager creatures get in their pointless lives."

Val clapped twice. "I will ensure the multiverse hails your name before the end of my life, Sir Overlord! However, I must regretfully inform you that the transporter is still a prototype. It'll be a short while before we can get it to pinpoint universes of our choosing." He stared at Ogenos, searching for a visible reaction, no doubt.

A minute passed before Val turned. "I shall leave the prototype with you, Sir Overlord. One of my soldiers will fetch for you when the transporter can be installed onto the mothership. If you need me for any reason at all, please do not hesitate to call on me!" With that, the Supreme General excused himself.

Ogenos sat there in silence, thinking about Val's words regarding the inferior lifeforms.

Meager was an understatement. Compared to him, those lower lifeforms were no more significant than that of space dust. And Val was beyond right. Their lives were pointless.

But they were happy.

That was the one constant he saw in those inferior beings throughout all his years of conquest. They were almost always content with their lot in life. Even those enslaved managed to make peace with their otherwise grim situation.

What were they doing differently from Ogenos? He had everything, and they had nothing! Yet, it didn't feel that way. In fact, it felt quite the opposite. But maybe that was his solution. Living the life of a commoner? He had never considered it before, but the more he thought about it, the more it made sense. At this point, he was willing to try anything.

But how would he go about it? His empire wouldn't just let him demote himself to the status of an inferior lifeform. In their eyes, he was a god; no one would dare treat him any differently.

I could go into hiding. He thought, quickly shaking his head at the idea. He'd be recognized wherever he went, for his image was as reaching as his influence. The thought of wearing a disguise to counter this crossed his mind, but no disguise in the world could conceal his aura for long. Eventually, he'd be found out.

Ogenos grumbled again, as he couldn't think of any ideas.

He went to face-palm himself, only to smack his head with a smooth orb. Ogenos flinched and looked down, forgetting the transporter was in his hand the whole time. He almost tossed the device away for breaking his train of thought, but then a new idea crept into his mind.

The transporter was meant to give the Malfadian Empire access to a plethora of undiscovered universes. Universes that had no knowledge of Ogenos's existence...

"Yes!" He shouted, shooting up from his throne and holding the transporter high. This was his key to a clean slate!

By crossing dimensions, he'd easily be able to integrate into a society or species similar to his own. He'd start at the bottom of the barrel and work his way up from there—assuming he wasn't complacent at the bottom.

Since the technology used on the transporter was new, it was unlikely his empire would be able to track him down immediately. Actually, they might not ever be able to find him since, with the multiverse being real, that also meant there was a near infinite number of universes to sift through.

Val and the others might be distraught after his departure, but they'd learn to get over it.

Now, all he had to do was figure out how the transporter worked. It shouldn't have been too hard, seeing as the symbols shifting around the orb were in the malfadian language.

He held the orb tightly and used two other hands to move the symbols. Val had mentioned there was not yet a mechanism that allowed the user to pick which universe to transport to, but Ogenos didn't care. Any universe was better than his own.

After a moment of moving the symbols, they suddenly stopped appearing. Ogenos sat back down in his seat, waiting with intoxicating anticipation.

What felt like years passed before the orb glowed brightly, illuminating the surrounding area.

Then it stopped. After that, nothing happened. Even the symbols stopped appearing.

"What?" Ogenos clicked his mandibles, confused. Had he done something wrong? If so, what was the correct way to use the transporter?

He asked himself a billion questions, shaking the orb like a fishbowl. Blue electricity sparked from the orb, shocking Ogenos and causing him to drop it. Though the electricity didn't hurt him, the suddenness of it startled him.

The transporter rolled down the many flights of steps until it reached the bottom. Ogenos looked at it, finally snapping himself out of his delusions.

"What am I doing?" A crackling noise emitted from his mandibles clicking together slowly.

He realized how stupid he must've looked... As if it would be that easy to abandon the life he knew. The transporter probably didn't work at all yet. It was only a prototype. Still, Ogenos couldn't help but let out a disappointed sigh.

He stood from his throne, and in the blink of an eye, he was on top of the transporter. Surprisingly, it wasn't cracked like he expected. Bellows sure knew how to make his inventions durable while simultaneously making them appear fragile.

Ogenos bent over, reaching for the fallen device, only for it to start vibrating. He hesitated and stood back, staring at the transporter in confusion.

Soon after the vibration started, it began glowing, but not like before. Unlike before, the brightness of the orb intensified with each passing second. Eventually, Ogenos had to look away and shield his eyes, but it did not help. The light would inevitably obscure his vision.

He waited a short minute, gradually feeling the light dim around him. Upon uncovering his eyes, he saw the transporter was gone... Everything was gone.

A cool breeze of air gently blew over Ogenos, making him shiver. "What...?" He looked around, finding himself in a suburban area of an unknown planetoid, standing in the center of a cement road.

He never made it a point to remember every single planet he'd conquered, but this one in particular felt unfamiliar. The buildings especially looked primitive by malfadian standards.

A low rumbling noise caught his attention, causing him to look down the paved road. In the distance, a vehicle of foreign design sped towards him. When it got close enough, it blared a horn so loud Ogenos nearly jumped out of his shell. Although he was sure the vehicle wouldn't hurt him in any way, his reflexes kicked in, and he jumped to the right onto a sidewalk.

The vehicle passed by without incident, though Ogenos quickly noticed it resembled a standard airion. The only difference was the airion wasn't hovering. It rolled across the road on four circular wheels, which would explain why its speed was considerably slow. Though, that wouldn't explain why its external lights were so bright.

He stared at the vehicle for a moment longer, then looked up to see an endless amount of stars dotting the black sky. "It's night?" He asked stupidly, watching the stars sparkle in the dark. There were so many of them—much more than he was used to seeing in the black void.

As his eyes shifted from each tiny speck, he caught sight of the big blue moon amongst the stars, staring back at him. He was getting *real* tired of seeing moons.

Ogenos stepped back, bumping into something solid. He turned, seeing it was a wooden sign. Strange letters were engraved in the wood.

He squinted, and after a moment of staring, he recognized the letters. They belonged to a long-dead language, once utilized by those hairless apes. What were they called again? Humans? He was pretty sure that was right.

Despite never studying the language, he was able to read the words. They spelled 'Wing Park.'

Behind the wooden sign was indeed a tiny park of some kind—one he often saw the inferior lifeforms take their young to. But like everything else he'd seen thus far, this park was primitive in design.

"What is this place?" He wondered aloud, then heard slight shuffling down the sidewalk.

Ogenos turned to see the silhouette of a bipedal figure in the distance. Although he couldn't see what they were in the dark, he could tell they were holding two bags.

He was about to demand they state their business, but a terrible headache overcame him abruptly. Then the dizziness hit, and he dropped to one knee in confusion. The silhouette had stopped in its tracks when Ogenos dropped to his knee.

After struggling to hold himself up, Ogenos flopped to the ground, exhausted. As his vision darkened, the last thing he saw was the silhouette dropping the plastic bags and rushing over to him.

Chapter 2

WELCOME TO TYRAN

Ogenos slowly opened his eyes, finding himself staring at a ceiling light. His mandibles clicked in confusion, followed by his hands feeling the ground, which turned out to be a carpeted floor.

"Hm..." He grumbled before sitting up groggily. His energy levels were down in the dumps, which was strange—He hadn't been this exhausted in a *long* time. Luckily, his dizziness had faded. Unluckily, the throbbing headache remained.

Ogenos groaned and rubbed the smooth surface of his bald head. After a few seconds of this, he paused. His helmet wasn't on him anymore.

He whipped around to survey his surroundings, half confused and half alert.

Judging by what he saw, he was in a residential area of an inferior lifeform. Admittedly, it looked fancier than he expected; it was much more spacious, too. There was a sofa, a TV, some chairs, a round wooden table, and even a little bar area in the back.

Ogenos spotted his helmet on the center of the table, sitting beside a bunch of other miscellaneous items he didn't care to examine. He stood and sauntered over to the table, placing the helmet back on his head.

Creaking footsteps suddenly came from behind while he adjusted his helmet. Ogenos looked over to where the noise came from, seeing a set of stairs hugging the wooden walls.

First, a shadow appeared; then, a figure stepped into view, holding something in their hands. Ogenos fully turned to face the figure, but they didn't notice him until they reached the bottom of the stairs. When they saw him standing, they flinched in shock and almost dropped whatever they were holding. "Good gracious!" They yelped, their tone masculine and firm.

The fear was warranted, considering Ogenos had an imposing aura. That, and the height difference between the two was enormous. While Ogenos stood at a towering height of seven feet and five inches, the entity before him was a meager five feet and ten inches.

To his surprise, the figure calmed down and spoke again. "I didn't expect you to wake up so soon. How are you doing? You alright? Need anything?"

This being wasn't afraid? That was... strange. No one ever spoke to Ogenos in such a casual manner. He wasn't sure how to feel about that.

And another thing, the creature clearly wasn't speaking malfadian, yet Ogenos understood it perfectly. Not only that, but the language sounded familiar. No, the creature *looked* familiar. He had interacted with this creature before, but from where?

Ogenos squinted his eyes and leaned forward, inspecting the creature's features.

It had a humanoid appearance, similar to Ogenos, but where he had a hard exoskeleton, it had fleshy skin that took on a palish color. They only possessed two eyes as opposed to his four; both were a hazel color. Additionally, they possessed a bunch of brown hair, primarily on their head and around their face.

Their clothing was no exception to their strangeness. Whereas Ogenos wore ceremonial armor, they wore nothing more than a red short-sleeved shirt, white shorts, and white tennis shoes. Equivalent to what he'd call rags.

Finally, it hit him. Ogenos knew what he was looking at. "You're human!"

The human tilted their head in confusion. "Yeah... I am," they said in a way that made it seem like Ogenos shouldn't have been surprised. Their tone made him feel stupid.

"The name's Steve! Steve Gale. You?"

Ogenos narrowed his eyes. "You—" He wanted to berate

the human, not only for speaking so casually to him, but for also making him feel like an imbecile. But he stopped himself.

"Wait." The unfamiliar planet, the primitive buildings and vehicles, the usage of a dead language—it could all only mean one thing: The transporter worked. Ogenos was in another universe.

The biggest giveaway was Steve—All humans had been driven to extinction in Ogenos's universe. They had to be, as they were the most defiant and aggressive out of any race he'd ever encountered before.

Ogenos being in a new universe would explain why he passed out. It wouldn't explain why he could suddenly read and understand their language. Actually, now that he thought about it, Steve could understand him perfectly. Was he even speaking malfadian anymore?

"Your name is Wait?" Steve asked, reminding Ogenos of his existence.

"No." He wanted to call Steve an idiot, but if he was really in a new world, then the last thing he should do was make an enemy. That's not what the average inferior organism would do...right?

After a long moment of silence, Ogenos figured it'd be fine if he used his real name. Since he was in a new universe, it's not like anyone would recognize him. "My name is Ogenos

Verum. You'd be wise to remember it." Before Steve could follow up with anything else, Ogenos pointed to the object in his hands. "Now answer me this: what is that?"

Steve looked down at his hands, then back up at Ogenos. "It's a pillow." He stepped up, handing him the pillow. "I tried laying you on the couch, but you were a bit too big for it. And I couldn't just have you sleeping on the floor with nothing, so I went to get you a pillow. I would've put you in a bed, but I was not about to drag you upstairs! You're really heavy, man." Ogenos took the pillow from Steve. The softness of it was incredible.

"I thought you'd be out for at least another couple of hours." He sounded puzzled, implying Ogenos hadn't been out for long. He'd then look over his shoulder at the stairs. "You... You didn't feel anything, did you?"

"Was I supposed to?"

"Oh, no! Just curious..." He nervously chuckled.

Ogenos followed Steve's gaze, seeing a few indents on the stairs and at the base of the steps.

Steve turned to see Ogenos looking and flailed his arms to get his attention. "S-So! What's up? Why'd you pass out? The Ragin' Bulls didn't get you, did they?"

"The...Ragin'...Bulls?"

"Yeah, that nasty gang of minotaurs."

"Minotaurs?"

Both men stared at each other blankly.

"Y-Yeah. Y'know? Part man, part bull?"

No, Ogenos did not know. "I was not assaulted by these raging bulls you speak of."

"Oh..." Steve tugged at the collar of his shirt. "Had too much to drink?"

Instead of letting Steve pelt him with questions, Ogenos gave him the answer outright. "It seems the atoms in my body were not accustomed to this new universe."

"H-Huh?"

Ogenos raised the pillow he was given and patted it with his two lower arms. The texture of it was enjoyable. "I guess I should've expected that. Even if this universe is an alternate version of my own, in theory, it is still fundamentally different from what I'm used to. Though, I never would've imagined I'd faint." He examined his upper right hand. "Luckily, it seems the atoms in my body have already adapted to this universe." There was some more silence as Steve gawked at him. "What?" He said, fishing for a response.

"So, you're like an alien from another universe?" Ogenos froze as Steve exposed his blunder.

Because of Steve's nonchalant attitude to Ogenos, he assumed space travel was common; therefore, so were other species. Even with their primitive design, he never once stopped to consider that this civilization was incapable of interstellar travel.

Now what was he to do? He already outed himself as a foreigner to the planet. His only option was to kill Steve and run. Though, even if his secret was kept safe, he'd have to hide out in the wilderness. His biology was far too different from mankind's to blend in with them... Now he wished he had packed a few supplies instead of leaving so hastily.

As if hearing his inner thoughts, Steve reacted to Ogenos's silence by flailing his arms once more. "O-Oh! Don't worry, I won't tell anyone your secret. Promise."

Ogenos perked up. "You can read minds?"

"Huh? No. I've just watched a lot of sci-fi flicks during my childhood, so I know an alien wouldn't want to be discovered. Like I said, I won't tell anyone your secret. Plus, you'll fit right in! You look like one of those insectoids. There's so many different kinds of them. No one's gonna bat an eye at you."

"You mean humans aren't the sole species of this planet?"

"You kiddin'? We got all kinds of races here! There's beast-people, cyclopes, ogres, hybrids...elves..." Steve shook his head. "There's a lot. Trust me, you'll fit right in!"

Steve's happy demeanor perturbed Ogenos. He was also astonished at how many species coexisted on one planet. For so many sentient creatures to develop on one planet *and not* battle each other for cultural dominance... This place really was a new universe.

Speaking of, "Where am I?"

"My house."

"I meant, what planet is this?" Ogenos clarified, annoyed.

"Oh." Steve chuckled nervously again. "Right, guess you would've meant that. Welcome to Tyran!"

Tyran... Ogenos couldn't help but feel like he'd heard that name from somewhere before. It probably wasn't important, so he pushed that thought to the back of his mind.

"Ogenos, right? If you don't mind me asking, why are you here?"

"You dragged me here."

Steve laughed. "I mean, why are you here on this planet? What brought you here?" Ogenos didn't respond immediately, as there were a million ways he could answer this question.

He could tell Steve the truth, but that would also mean giving him context—context that would reveal his many, many atrocities. He could also just give Steve the short version and say he's a conqueror who retired, but in his experience, inferior lifeforms frowned at the sight of a conqueror. There was no doubt in Ogenos's mind that the creatures here wouldn't like him based on his former title.

Ogenos did the one thing he could logically do in a situation like this. "I'm a traveler, but my days of wandering are over. I've been searching for a place to call home. While unexpected, I'm thinking Tyran might be that place." He lied.

Steve eyed him up and down. Ogenos wasn't sure if the glare was suspicious or not. He got his answer when he saw Steve's eyes light up like a newborn's upon discovering the world for the first time.

"Tyran is a great place to live in! We got so many sights, activities, people, and food! Sure, it gets extremely cold one season and simmering hot the next, but we manage."

Luckily, he believed Ogenos's lie. Still, there were a few problems with his situation. "You say that, but you forget I am unaccustomed to this world." He half-said that to let Steve know what he was thinking, but he mainly said it for himself. Ogenos hadn't realized until now that if he wanted to start from the bottom and live the life of an inferior life-form, he first needed to learn how they lived.

"Oh, I got you covered! I can teach you all about this place."

Ogenos paused. "You'd do that?"

"Yeah! I mean, I already dragged you to my house. Plus, I got nothing better to do, so I might as well be your guide."

"Is dragging people to another's living quarters a common thing done here?"

A sweat bead formed on Steve's forehead. "W-Well, no.

Not really. We call that kidnapping, actually... B-But you were unconscious! Normally, you'd call the police, but the Ragin' Bulls sometimes roam these streets. I couldn't just leave you there."

"But if that's not something that's normally done, why do it?"

Steve made an awkward facial expression, then rubbed the back of his head. "I just like helping people. Y'know?"

Ogenos fought the urge to give Steve a skeptical look. He could tell the human was hiding something from him. As much as he wanted to press for answers, the situation was turning in his favor—Not only did he land on a planet with a diverse population he could easily blend in with, but he also unintentionally netted himself a guide who could show him both, how Tyran works and how to live life as an inferior being—Ogenos would be the biggest fool in the multiverse to ruin this.

Besides, Steve looked no stronger than an infant malfade. Should push come to shove, Ogenos could easily just kill him.

"Alright, then." He said, clicking his mandibles attentively.

Steve smiled. "You kinda dropped in at the perfect time 'cause I'm off work tomorrow. I can show you 'round the city then."

"That sounds acceptable."

"Awesome. One more thing, does your species sleep or...?"

"We do."

"Okay, great! Well, seeing as you've got nowhere else to stay, I'll get the guest bedroom set up for you and—"

Ogenos raised one free hand, shaking his head. "No need. This place looks adequate enough."

"R-Really? You sure you're fine with sleeping in the base-ment?"

Ogenos nodded. Truthfully, he would've wanted Steve to set up that guest bedroom for him, but he felt it was too sim-ilar to how his servants always prepared his private cham-bers right before bed. He did not want to live a life that was even close to resembling his old one. This was supposed to be a fresh start from the past, not a reminder.

"Well, if you say so." Steve stood there awkwardly, staring at Ogenos for a moment too long. "I-I'm gonna go tuck in for the night. Sleep tight, don't let the bedbugs bite."

"Bugs?" Ogenos clicked.

"Oh, sorry. That must be offensive. Uh... Sweet dreams!" He went up the steps, stopping about halfway before turn-ing back to Ogenos. "Rest up well. Tomorrow is gonna be exciting! Trust me, you're gonna love it here!" He declared before disappearing from view.

Ogenos looked at where Steve last was, then turned back

to the pillow given to him. After a second of staring, he held it with one hand and patted it with his other three. It was much softer than he expected, not to mention calming to the touch. He couldn't stop touching it. "This is nice."

Chapter 3
A MALL AND A TYRANT

The next day came, and as morning arrived, so too did an enthusiastic Steve, whom Ogenos was quickly awoken by.

As his eyes adjusted, he saw Steve wearing clothing different from the ones he wore last night. Though he didn't care much about the wardrobe change, he noticed the clothes looked much neater. Smelled nicer, too.

Steve hurriedly dragged Ogenos out of the house and into the warm outdoors. The latter then spotted something parked next to Steve's house. "What is this...?" He stared, soon recognizing the object as a primitive transport vehicle, similar to the one he had seen previously, just more robust and red.

"It's an SUV! You guys have those where you're from, don't you?" Steve replied.

"We have airions. Not SUVs."

"Oohhhh...." Steve said awkwardly, clapping his hands to keep the silence away. "Well, this is all I've got. Sure, it's used, but I snagged it for a pretty sweet deal! Come on, get in." He gestured and went to get inside.

Ogenos resisted the urge to blast Steve and his sorry excuse for a transport vehicle away. "This is how the inferior lifeforms speak to each other, Ogenos. Surely, you can handle this much..." He muttered before joining Steve inside the SUV.

"Nice, right?" Steve smiled, proudly presenting his transport.

It smelled weird, felt uncomfortably warm, and looked unsatisfactory. Steve was lucky Ogenos could even fit inside something so small, to begin with. For what it's worth, the dark interior colors were pleasing to the eyes.

"Adequate," Ogenos mumbled, staring ahead through the small front window.

"Yeah, I knew you'd like it! Also, sorry if it's cramped. My friends aren't usually as big as you."

Friends... Ogenos was familiar with the term. Many inferior organisms used it to describe another inferior organism they were cordial with.

Steve's use of the term confirmed one thing: Tyran had terms, and possibly other concepts, that Ogenos could refer and relate to. This would make integration into Steve's civilization a little easier.

Suddenly, a thought crossed his mind. One that made him suspicious. "Tell me, Steve. If you had this transport unit at your disposal, why not use it last night?"

"I was only getting a few things. Besides, the convenience store was just down the road."

"You weren't at all worried about...what was it again? Oh. Those raging minotaurs?"

Steve's brow twinged. "Well, gas is pretty expensive nowadays, so I think it was well worth the risk."

"Gas?"

"Right, you're from another planet... It's what we use as fuel for our cars."

Cars—that's what these primitive transports are called. Interesting. Ogenos noted as Steve began babbling off about details relating to his personal vehicle, details that Ogenos didn't care for in the slightest.

Eventually, he finally started the car, and the two were off. That didn't keep Steve from talking—about what Ogenos did not know. He tuned him out and focused on the passing environment.

The first thing to catch his attention was the green flora, followed by the clear blue sky. Once he saw the bright yellow sun, that's when it hit him. This planet was the spitting image of that resort world he conquered centuries ago. Funnily enough, it belonged to the humans back when they were still around.

Could this really be an alternate universe? No, it couldn't

be. He doesn't recall the planet being named Tyran, nor it having this much...life...

The first signs of active life were small brown rodent-like critters jumping around in the grass and scurrying up in the trees. The next were small avians either flying high in the sky or staying perched on a few buildings.

Then there were the humans and the hybrids of humans. If they weren't one or the other, they were a humanoid of some kind. Some looked familiar; others looked completely alien. They were everywhere.

"Enjoying the sights?" Steve said, forcing Ogenos to come up with a response.

"Your planet is very...abundant." He turned back to Steve, who gave him a light chuckle.

"Yeah, we got all types of people. Especially here in Valentina City."

"City? You call this a city?"

"Well, uh, yeah? What would you call it?"

Ogenos looked back out the window and nearly shouted *'What!'*

He had taken his eyes off their surroundings for less than a minute, and somehow, they had left the suburban area and entered a more urbanized landscape.

Enormous skyscrapers towered over them, similar to the metropolises back home. They passed by many shops and alleys, and now there were four times as many people as there were before.

"Never mind," Ogenos muttered, hurriedly changing subjects. "What did you mean by especially here?"

"Well, Valentina is big. Like, really big! It's one of the most populated cities in the whole world. In fact, it has the most diversity out of anyplace else."

Before Ogenos could get a word in, Steve rambled once again. "You know, it used to be called Angel City! It was twice as big then. But after it got destroyed, they ended up down-scaling it for safety reasons."

"How was it destroyed?" Ogenos swiftly asked.

"Oh, a tyrant came through and wrecked the whole place."

"You mean a conqueror razed the city down?"

Steve looked at him perplexed, then focused on the road ahead. "Sorry, I keep forgetting you're not from this world. Not sure what a conqueror is, but the tyrants here are terrible monsters."

"Wait. You don't know what a conqueror is?"

"Um, no. Is that like a creature or something?" Ogenos stared at Steve, contemplating how he didn't know what a conqueror was. His answer implied he lacked even the basic concept of what a conqueror was.

Did the many evolving species never clash for superiority? Assuming the developing cultures on Tyran always coexisted in peace, that'd explain Steve's ignorance. Still, the possibility of that being the case on Tyran, let alone any planet, was extremely unlikely.

Then again, with the discovery of the multiverse, it wasn't exactly impossible...

"Forget it," Ogenos said, turning back to the skyscrapers. "So a single monster destroyed a city twice as big as Valentina?" If that was true, then the defenses of Tyran must've been horrendous.

"Y-Yeah, but don't worry! That tyrant was a rare type. Plus, protocols have been put in place to keep civilians safe from stuff like that... Not that we've ever had to use them. No tyrant has ever attacked Valentina City." It seemed Steve mistook Ogenos's question as a sign of fear and did his best to reassure him. Ogenos just nodded passively. "Besides, even if a tyrant did attack, the hunters would be on them like bread and butter."

Hunters? That interested Ogenos. "And what are hunters?"

"Only the coolest people to ever exist! They specialize in taking down tyrants and protecting the people! They're basically our military." Steve praised, unable to contain his excitement. That's when he gave Ogenos a quick glance. "Which is why we're gonna have to get you a change of clothes."

Ogenos looked down at himself. "What is wrong with my attire?"

"You're dressed like a hunter! Sort of..." Steve looked around before accelerating the car. "It's illegal to pose as one without a license. But don't worry, I know just the place."

The place Steve had in mind wasn't quite what Ogenos expected. Usually, when one wants a change of clothes, you go to a shop that specializes in clothes. Not a large mall.

If Ogenos remembered Steve's ramblings correctly, the place was called Valentine Mall—very original.

Names aside, he found himself following Steve around like a leashed pet—which was humiliating in its own right. It couldn't be helped. If he wanted to learn how to live like the inferiors around him, then his first objective was to acquire a new set of clothes.

Steve only made the process more complicated by wanting to get clothes for different activities. It didn't help that he took Ogenos into multiple different stores, and since the mall was massive, they'd done a lot of walking.

On the bright side, Steve was right about one thing: Ogenos didn't stick out. All around them were creatures of varying shapes and sizes. Some flew, others skittered, and some even rolled. A few were like giants, dwarfing even Ogenos. Others were only as big as his toes.

The mall's shops also mimicked this, as some were perched high above so only the fliers or wall climbers could reach them; others had entrances so small that not even an infant malfade could fit through.

Eventually, Steve decided he had purchased enough clothes for Ogenos—not before forcing him to try on a million different pairs, of course. Surprisingly, all the clothes Steve found fit his physiology almost perfectly.

Even though their shopping had concluded, Steve wanted to make *extra* sure he had everything, so they stayed put at a nearby bench as he went through the different articles of clothing. "Alright, let's see here. I got you everyday attire, formal attire, pajamas, golf attire..."

Ogenos did a double-take. "Golf...?"

"Yeah, golf. Trust me, you'll love it!"

Ogenos had never heard of anything called golf. That must've been a Tyran-exclusive activity.

"O-M-G. Is that Stevie?" A sudden high-pitched voice called out, grating Ogenos's nonexistent ears. He turned to see where the insufferable noise came from.

His eyes landed on another pale-skinned human, who was somehow even shorter than Steve. They wore a short green dress, and as they approached, their black heels clicked and clacked against the ground.

Their hot-pink-covered lips curled into a creepy smile. "What are the odds I'd run into you again!" They snickered, crossing their smooth arms underneath their chest, which was unusually large compared to Steve's.

It caught Ogenos off guard until he remembered humans were a dioecious species, like malfadian. Unlike malfadian, their sexes weren't as distinctly different from one another. At least, not at a glance.

The woman flicked her long blonde hair to the side, staring at Steve with baby-blue eyes. "How've you been?" she asked, and her ears suddenly fidgeted.

It was then that Ogenos noticed her ears weren't the same as Steve's. They were narrow and much longer. One of which was even pierced with a golden ring that shimmered under the mall's artificial lights.

"Steve, you know this long-eared human?" Ogenos whispered, not wanting the lady to know he was ignorant of her.

Steve hadn't sat up from his kneeling position, so his back was still turned to Ogenos and the woman. His whole body was tense, and his breaths were shaky. Was he...scared? No ... The emotion he displayed seemed more like anger.

"Yeah, I know her. But she isn't human." Steve murmured. "No human could be as wicked as her."

"Not human?"

"She's an elf." He clarified with a shaky sigh.

Finally, Steve got up and turned to face the elf lady. Upon seeing his face, her own curled into a twisted look of satisfaction—one that even gave Ogenos the creeps. "Aww. You don't look too happy to see me, Stevie. What's wrong? Are you still mad?" She snickered again, practically taunting him.

Ogenos glanced downward, noticing Steve's fists were clenched tightly. He half expected Steve to haul off and punch the woman. That's what he would've done if he had to listen to her obnoxious voice for more than a minute.

Instead, Steve just gave her a stern look. "What do you want, Maya?"

"What? I can't bump into an old friend anymore? I mean, it's not like I purposefully sought you out." She rolled her eyes with a scoff. "But hey! Since you're here, I can finally introduce you to that handsome rogue I told you all about," Maya said with glee.

Suddenly, a large man-beast appeared out of nowhere, now standing right beside Maya.

This creature was dissimilar to Steve and Maya, boasting a muscular physique, black fur, and a height equivalent to Ogenos's. Their face was oddly shaped, possessing two gray eyes, a nose ring, and two horns, with the left being chipped at the tip. Their clothing was no better either, as all they seemed to have on was a red unzipped leather jacket and leggings.

"This is—"

"Samuel Kage. Yeah, I know. He's the minotaur you wouldn't shut up about!" Steve said in a raised voice, unable to contain his anger towards Maya.

A puff of smoke escaped Samuel's nostrils as he gave Steve a death stare. In that same instance, Steve realized his mistake, and to show he did, his face morphed into an expression of fear.

"Who told you to speak to my girl like that?" Samuel took one heavy step forward, stomping his hooves on the floor. Steve jumped back, nearly falling over all the bags of clothes.

"Now, now, Sam. There's no need to make a scene. We both know he won't try anything with you around." Maya rubbed Samuel's arm lovingly, causing his bushy tail to sway. He stepped back, and finally, Ogenos's presence was noticed.

"So, Stevie. Who's your little friend?" Maya asked smugly.

Steve looked at Ogenos worriedly. If his body language was anything to go by, he clearly didn't want to answer her question. But his fear of Samuel was much too noticeable. "He's—"

Ogenos put a hand out to stop Steve from continuing. He refused to let Steve answer her question, partially because he knew he'd rattle on and give her information she didn't need to know. "My name is Ogenos Verum. That is all you need to know." He answered, crossing all four of his arms.

Samuel must've taken offense to how Ogenos spoke to Maya, as he got riled up again. "Hey, buddy. She wasn't talking to you."

"I don't care."

Steve's eyes widened as he whipped his head to Ogenos.

Maya let go of Samuel's arm, followed by the beast stepping up to Ogenos's face. "Sorry, what was that? I don't think I heard you properly."

Ogenos didn't move an inch, although he wanted to due to the horrific smell coming from Samuel's mouth. "Then pay attention. I dislike repeating myself." He said loudly, keeping his arms crossed. "I said I don't care."

Steve jumped in between the two titans, laughing nervously. "Wow! I think we're getting off on the wrong foot here. Uh, give me a second." He said politely while gently pushing on Ogenos's chest. It seemed like Steve wanted to talk, so he backed away from Samuel willingly.

"Hey, Ogenos, buddy? I appreciate you standing your ground and all, but Samuel is not the minotaur to mess with!"

"And why not?"

"Remember that Ragin' Bulls gang I told you about last

night?"

"What about it?"

"Well, you see, the funny thing is—*Samuel's their leader!*"

"Is that supposed to scare me?"

"Yes! A lot, actually!"

"Well, it doesn't." Ogenos stepped right back up to Samuel, allowing him and Maya to hear them again.

"Ogenos, Ogenos! Look, I don't mean to doubt your strength or anything, but Samuel is seriously not a guy you wanna fight. He'll flatten you!"

Ogenos chuckled at Steve's warning. "He's free to try. However, if he'd like to live a long and fulfilling life, I wouldn't recommend it."

More smoke puffed from Samuel's nose. Finally, he had enough and pushed Steve to the side with ease. He reared back a fist, about to make the first move.

Suddenly, all the lights in the mall started flashing red, making Samuel stop in his tracks.

"Attention all shoppers. This is a code B emergency." A feminine automated voice blared throughout the mall. If the flashing lights didn't catch everyone's attention, the voice sure did. "I repeat, this is a code B emergency. Please evacuate the building immediately. This is not a drill."

There was a brief pause as the collective masses processed everything. Then, the whole mall was abruptly thrown into chaos. Everybody screamed and scrambled to the nearest exit.

"Babe!" Maya squealed, hugging Samuel's arm tightly.

He hoisted Maya into his arms instantly, cradling her like a newborn. Afterward, he gave Ogenos a long, aggressive stare, possibly engraving his physical features into his head. "You got lucky." He huffed. Then, like those around them, he dashed towards the closest exit.

Ogenos saw his fleeing as cowardice. He could've easily thrown his flimsy punch, regardless of the situation happening before them. Then again, it was probably for the best. He didn't want to waste any energy on a lifeform as insignificant as Samuel anyway.

"Ogenos, we gotta go!" Steve shouted in a panic, tugging on Ogenos's arm desperately. The tone in his voice held the fear of a dozen people, but Ogenos was unbothered.

"What's the rush? I thought you wanted to check your acquired possessions." He reminded.

"Did you not hear the announcement?!" Steve said, looking at him as if he were crazy.

Ogenos *did* hear the message, but he was not that concerned—partly because he didn't understand what it meant. All he knew was an evacuation had been ordered. That alone probably should've sparked some semblance of alert in him, but he didn't feel as though his life was in danger.

"I feel the need to remind you that I am not yet accustomed to this world," Ogenos stated calmly.

Steve fidgeted in response, stifling a scream. "A tyrant is on the way! A B-Tier tyrant!"

"But I thought you said no tyrant has ever attacked this city before?"

"Until today!" Steve yelled, grabbing Ogenos with both hands and tugging harder. "We have to go! Now!!" Even with all his strength, Ogenos didn't budge an inch.

He watched as Steve put everything into pulling him. If Steve wasn't his guide, he would've had him executed for being so grabby. Oh, but executions probably weren't a common thing for inferior beings to do to those they disliked... Ogenos would have to work on not resorting to those thoughts.

That aside, he still didn't see what the fuss was about. "Steve, you are over..." He looked away, only to pause at their surroundings. The mall's alarms had been loud—so loud that he thought they were muffling out the people's screams. In reality, no one was there. "...reacting..."

Ogenos wasn't sure when the screams faded, but the panicking crowd was no longer present. All the shops had either been vacated or locked down, maybe even both, which left the once-packed mall with only him and Steve.

Maybe Steve's panicking was warranted.

Just as Ogenos finally realized how serious the situation was, the ground rumbled faintly. "Oh no." Steve quivered and stopped tugging on Ogenos.

A massive plume of smoke shot out from the ground in front of them as something gigantic broke from underneath, emitting a shockwave that knocked Steve clean off his feet and sent chunks of debris everywhere.

The debris destroyed various shops and damaged the walls of the mall. Ogenos held firm as his cape blew violently, staring directly at the forming cloud of debris. He wanted to get a better look at this B-Tier tyrant.

The tyrant must've read his mind, as it swung a large appendage to clear away the smoke, revealing its figure.

The beast was huge, making Ogenos and Steve look like tiny insects in comparison. Despite its height, it was still small enough to fit within the mall. Steve made it seem like the tyrant could flatten the whole city by stepping on it.

Another interesting feature Ogenos noticed was how closely the tyrant resembled a creature from his home planet.

"N-No way..." Steve stammered, paralyzed. "W-What's a crabor doing so far inland? T-They never leave the ocean..."

Wow. The tyrant even comes from the sea like the creature it reminded him of! "This crabor reminds me of a shellfish back on Malfada. I believe Val has one as a pet." Yes, he could see it so clearly now! This crabor tyrant was the spitting image of those dark purple little crustaceans—only the tyrant was red and white in color, not to mention much bigger.

As if taking his absentmindedness as an insult, the crabor let out a deep crackling roar and reared one of its massive pinchers back. When it lunged for the attack, Steve's eyes widened. "OGENOS! WATCH—" A resounding clank cut his words off like a cleaver to meat.

The tyrant's pinchers collided with Ogenos, and Steve felt the surging gust of air from its attack, which made him slide backward a little. It moved fast, much faster than one might expect from a heavily armored tyrant. Unfortunately for the crabor, it did not move fast enough.

Steve watched in awe as Ogenos stopped the tyrant's thrust-like attack with a single palm. Moreover, the creature's pincher shook heavily, like it was struggling to push Ogenos back. Ogenos, on the other hand, was so unbothered by the tyrant that he turned away from it, looking to Steve.

"Did you say something? I wasn't listening." He said casually, eliciting another crackling roar from the tyrant. Ogenos raised one finger. "One moment." He turned back to the tyrant, flicking it with the same finger and a groan of annoyance. "Annoying pest."

At first, the flick didn't seem to do anything. Then, suddenly, the tip of the tyrant's pincher trembled and crackled. Large cracks formed at the tip of the pincher, traveling down the tyrant's arm and spreading throughout the rest of its body. Each crack only grew bigger and wider than the last—It was as if an invisible force was applying immense pressure on it from all sides.

The tyrant roared in what Ogenos assumed was pain. After a short delay, its armor shattered in an explosive display; its purple fluorescent flesh and green guts exploded outward from its back, coating much of the area behind it in its innards.

"Now, as you were saying?" Ogenos turned back to Steve, disregarding everything that just happened.

"...What..." Steve croaked in disbelief as he stared behind Ogenos.

All that remained of the crabor was one of its eight long legs.

Chapter 4

THE CALM LIFE

To say Steve was flabbergasted would be an understatement. He looked shell-shocked.

Ogenos was slightly confused by his astonishment. In his eyes, a wild beast attacked him, and he simply defended himself. Was it not the standard thing to do on Tyran?

"You... You killed a B-Tier tyrant..." Steve whimpered, standing to his feet while wobbling.

"I deemed it a threat. Was I wrong to kill it?"

"Wrong to kill it? Ogenos, you just saved thousands of lives! Mine included!"

Ogenos studied Steve's face, seeing his shock still remained. "You don't look too pleased. In fact, you look rather surprised," he pointed out, making a small clicking noise.

"How can I not be surprised?! You killed a B-Tier tyrant with just a flick of your finger!"

"Is that not normal?"

"Normal? If that was normal for everyone, tyrants would be the least of our problems! Those things destroy cities,

Ogenos!" Steve let out a long sigh, reeling himself in. "It would've taken a group of hunters to take down that crabor. With strength like that, you'd be on par with an alpha-class hunter!"

Ogenos clicked his mandibles together, feeling irritation swell within him. This time, the source of his agitation came not from Steve, but himself.

How could he be so foolish? He deemed the tyrant a threat and took it upon himself to kill it, but didn't stop to consider that's not something the average inferior would, or even could, do. Honestly, he should've taken the hint when the masses were running for their meager lives.

"With power like that, you'd easily become a top-ranking hunter, no doubt! The Hunter Agency would love to have you!"

Ogenos perked up. "Hunter Agency?"

"O-Oh, right. I never did explain that, did I?" Steve paused, as if pondering his next choice of words. "Remember how I said hunters were like the military? Well, the Hunter Agency is like the government that governs them."

Of course that's what the Hunter Agency was. Ogenos should've just taken an educated guess. Though, that gave him an idea. "Tell me, is it considered a standard to become a hunter?"

Steve's eyes sparkled with happiness for a moment, but

his smile faltered quickly. "No, not really. It takes a special kind of person to be a hunter. Like you! You should sign up to be one."

Despite Steve painting the hunters in a positive light, Ogenos did not share his eagerness in becoming one. "No."

Steve paused. Then, his face scrunched up in confusion. It was almost as if he hadn't heard Ogenos correctly or, at the very least, believed he hadn't. "N-No?" He repeated questioningly.

Ogenos nodded to confirm he had heard correctly. "That's what I said."

"W-Why not?"

"Doesn't sound worthwhile." He stated; truly, that's what Ogenos believed.

Initially, he thought the organisms of Tyran would be a match for him. But after that run-in with the B-Tier tyrant, it was clear he still far out-classed the creatures in this universe—or at least on this planet. Besides, his goal wasn't to climb the ranks in a new hierarchy, even if the climb differed slightly from the last.

"What do you mean it doesn't sound worthwhile?? Think of all the lives you could save! The difference you could make!" Steve could not comprehend how Ogenos could be so content with not abusing the power he so obviously wielded.

Little did Steve know, Ogenos already had his experience of abusing his power; it was not as thrilling as it sounded. But he couldn't just tell Steve that. Even if he did, it was doubtful that Steve's feeble mind would understand anyway.

Ogenos paused in thought, clicking his mandibles together absentmindedly. "I'm tired." He answered, somewhat truthfully. "Wandering from galaxy to galaxy gets exhausting after a while. I just wish to rest and live the calm life. Can one not do so?"

Steve paused, a look of realization overtaking his face. Ogenos wasn't sure what he realized, but whatever it was, it softened his expression. "Alright... I understand. I won't push the subject any further."

The genuine sincerity in Steve's voice caught Ogenos off guard. He hadn't expected his half-lie to work so effortlessly. Was Steve just that dumb?

Before he could lose himself in his thoughts, Ogenos and Steve were jerked to reality by the loud sounds of various vehicles pulling up from outside. "Shoot, we gotta go!" Steve announced, scrambling to grab the bags of purchased clothes.

"What's with the rush? Didn't I deal with the threat?"

"You did, but the hunters are here. I don't know about you, but I'd rather not be the one to explain how there are two uninjured people next to a B-Tier tyrant's corpse."

Ogenos couldn't argue with that, so he helped grab the remaining bags, then quickly followed Steve through one of the many exits. Luckily, the hunters hadn't surrounded the mall, so they slipped out undetected.

As they left, ironclad vehicles pulled into the parking lot, and armored creatures varying in shape and size piled out of the vehicles and into the mall, all of whom were geared for war.

On the drive back to Steve's house, all Ogenos could think about was the tyrant he obliterated. Although clearly an animal, the tyrant didn't seem like a natural beast compared to the rodent-like critters and small avians from earlier. What were they, exactly?

"Steve."

"Yeah, Genos?"

"Refrain from calling me that," Ogenos said sternly before continuing. "These tyrants. What are they?"

Steve raised a brow, keeping his eyes trained on the road ahead. "Well, they're monsters."

"I remember you saying that. But I mean, what are they exactly? They don't seem to fit with the life I've observed thus far."

"I guess I can see why you'd think that. If I'm being honest, they're still an enigma to us as well." Steve lightly shifted in his seat, only to stop the vehicle at a red light. Ogenos didn't quite understand why he stopped, since it allowed the cars ahead to go.

Either way, Steve turned to him. "History shows that tyrants have been with us for...well, ever. Yet, we don't know where they come from. They rarely attack each other and always show zero interest in other wildlife... It's like the only thing they want to hunt is us."

"Well, if my kind were hunted by you, that's how I'd retaliate."

"But that's the thing! They hunted us first! It's the only reason the Hunter Agency was created."

"And who created that?"

"No clue, but it's managed by some guy called 'The Director.' Honestly? That's a pretty cool name."

The light ahead of them changed from red to green, and soon enough, they were moving again.

"So this director chooses who's best suited to become a hunter?"

"Well, no. You submit an application to the agency detailing what you can do, and if they like what they see, you go to a testing center for evaluation. Pass that, then they send you to one of several hunter academies. You stay there a few years, and if you pass with flying colors, you become a hunter! That's when the director chooses which class you're best suited for."

"Class... yes. I recall you saying I could become an alpha-class hunter."

"With your raw strength alone? Absolutely!"

"Out of curiosity, what are the other classes of a hunter?"

"There's five." Steve raised his fingers one by one as he went down the list. "First, you got the novice-class hunters. Those are basically the newbies. Then there's the omega-class hunters, who are slightly more reliable than the novice-class. Beta-class hunters are the people you really want for protection. Though, in times of crisis, the alpha-class hunters are your go-to."

Ogenos clicked happily upon seeing alpha-class hunters were amongst the strongest of the other classes. That's when he noticed Steve only held four fingers up. "That's only four classes. You said there were five?"

"Five there is indeed. If you're looking for true hunters, then look no further than the apex-class!" Steve said energetically, pumping his fist in the air. "They're the best of the best! No one but The Director can touch 'em!"

Ogenos crossed his four arms and grumbled. "What's so special about the apex-class?"

"Uh, only that they represent everything the Hunter Agency stands for! Shoot, they're basically treated like royalty, and for good reason. Everyone in that class is in a tier of their own! The agency only ever allows ten at a time. I mean, to be fair, there's not many other hunters who could take on multiple high-tier tyrants single-handedly. That alone warrants respect."

Ogenos grumbled some more, severely disappointed that Steve didn't think he was apex-class material. He masked his disappointment by switching topics. "Speaking of high-tier tyrants, you referred to that crabor tyrant as a B-Tier. Was that a high-tier tyrant?"

Steve nodded. "Yep, though it was more on the lower end of high-tier. They're still very dangerous, though."

"What are the other tiers?"

"Well, there's a bit more tyrant tiers than there are classes of hunters, all of which have their own specifications and dangers. But to keep it short, for low-tiers, you have the E's, D's, and C's. And for the high-tiers, you have the B's, A's, and S's."

"If the B-Tiers can level cities, then I presume the A and S-Tiers are that much more deadly?"

"Oh, by far. But don't worry. B-Tiers are the only ones you see nowadays. A-Tiers are rare, and no one has seen an S-Tier in centuries! They might've gone extinct."

"Alright, but you said a tyrant has never attacked this city before, and that just happened."

Steve winced. "Er, well... let's just chalk it up to bad luck. Better yet, consider it a very unique welcome to Tyran."

"...Well, it was the first time a monster on a foreign world has ever dared to attack me."

"See! A very unique welcome." Steve made it sound like the welcome was anything but life-threatening—At least it would've been were it not for Ogenos's power. Though, for what it was worth, killing that tyrant was... enjoyable.

Upon arriving at Steve's residence, the two found themselves in an area of the house he referred to as the living room.

Ogenos noted how much smaller it was compared to when he last saw it, but then again, he wasn't really given the time to examine it until now. Were all human homes this small? No—it was much more feasible that Steve's humble abode was simply tiny compared to the grandiose rooms Ogenos was used to.

"Woo, boy." Steve stretched after placing the bags on his sofa. "Talk about an eventful first day! First time in the city, and you've already met your first tyrant. What do you say we change into something more comfy?" He looked over his shoulder, meeting Ogenos's gaze.

"Comfy can wait." His mandibles clicked. "You promised to show me how infe—" He stopped himself, remembering inferior lifeforms don't typically address each other as inferior lifeforms. "You promised to show me how people like yourself live. To... what was it you said? Show me the ropes?"

Steve made an odd clicking noise with his tongue. "Ah, I did say that."

"Then let us start. We've ran your errands and bested your tyrants. It is time to show me how one lives life...normally."

Steve tapped his chin, looking around the living room. "I guess the first thing to start on would be chores. You...know what those are, right?"

"Chores? You mean minuscule tasks?"

"Well, that's one way to look at 'em. But I like to think of chores as a way to build character." He gestured for Ogenos to follow as he exited the living room and entered another area of the house.

Right next to the basement entrance was a room with a smooth stone floor and marbled walls. Within were a few contraptions, all unrecognizable to Ogenos.

"We'll start with my favorite: laundry!" Steve said excitedly.

Next to one of the contraptions was a white bucket filled

with clothes thrown haphazardly inside. A strange smell permeated from the bucket.

"Yes...laundry..." Ogenos repeated awkwardly.

Steve turned, watching Ogenos stare at the bucket of dirty clothes. "Do you know how to do laundry?" he asked hesitantly.

Ogenos thought about lying, but figured that would be counterproductive to his goals. Swallowing his pride, he shook his head.

Steve only smiled in response. "It's really simple. Here, lemme show you."

Chapter 5

HAPPY BURGERS

As it turns out, laundry wasn't the only thing Ogenos didn't know how to do.

Organization, cooking, cleaning, and every other skill was a foreign concept to him. It's like he never had to work a day in his life!

Steve couldn't really blame him, though. Being a war hero and saving dozens of people must've been tiring, at least mentally. Ogenos never explicitly said it, so it was just an assumption on Steve's part—but him being a retired hero *had* to be the case. How else could he casually face that tyrant without showing even an ounce of fear? Not to mention his strength was through the roof!

Steve had no idea what kind of glamorous lifestyle Ogenos left behind, and despite his age being an enigma, it sounded like he had been at it for a long time. Maybe he just wanted a long-awaited break for all the hard work he'd done.

In any case, who was Steve, a man who had never lived that kind of life, to tell Ogenos to continue fighting the good fight? Everyone was entitled to retirement, regardless of their profession! And as far as he was concerned, Ogenos had put in more than enough time.

Therefore, Steve gladly taught Ogenos all he needed to know about chores. It took a bit since Ogenos didn't want to learn the next thing until he got the previous task down pat. Luckily, it didn't take all night.

That didn't stop Steve from nearly sleeping in until the afternoon. Had it not been for his alarm, he would've never noticed the rays of morning light creep into his window.

He would've liked to stay home to continue giving Ogenos some guidance, but unfortunately, he had other obligations.

Groggily, Steve woke himself up and bathed quickly. He'd then slip on his work uniform, which consisted of a red buttoned t-collared shirt and blue-colored pants held up by a yellow belt. Of course, he couldn't forget his yellow-striped blue shoes.

Before he rushed out of the room, he spotted the last piece of his uniform sitting atop his dresser: a small badge resembling a smiling burger. He swiped it, swiftly clipping it onto his shirt. "That should do it." He told himself before heading downstairs.

Steve was promptly greeted by Ogenos in the living room. No longer did he have his purple-colored armor on. Instead, he was dressed in casual clothing.

Steve smiled in satisfaction over his choice of clothing. He was right to stick with the purple theme Ogenos had going on, for he looked much better in the clothes than he ever did in the armor.

Ogenos was currently sweeping the carpeted floor with a broom. Steve couldn't help but smile at his attempt to clean the place. "You might want to use a vacuum for that," he announced, revealing his presence.

Ogenos stared at him for a moment, then back down at the broom. "In hindsight, that would be best..." He clicked. Steve could've sworn he heard a hint of embarrassment in his tone.

Don't sweat it, Ogenos. It happens to the best of us. Steve chuckled.

Ogenos looked like he was about to say something else, but paused upon seeing Steve's clothes. The alien gave him a quick glance up and down. "My stars!"

"W-What?" Steve asked in genuine concern, having never heard such shock in Ogenos's tone before.

"What are you wearing?!" He pointed.

"It's my work uniform?"

"Unacceptable. It is an affront. Remove it."

"Can't. It's mandatory."

"That's legal?!"

Steve laughed at how astounded Ogenos was. For someone who lacked many decipherable facial features, he was very expressive. The people back wherever he came from must've loved him.

That said, it became apparent there were plenty of things Ogenos didn't fully understand, such as a job.

"Well, you know, Ogenos, this is what happens when you have a job."

He looked up and made that insect-like clicking noise again. "A simple job has you bound to that atrocity you call a uniform?"

It seemed that Ogenos at least knew what a job was, so that left less for Steve to explain. "Afraid so."

"To the pit of eternal flames with that job, then! You can always find another."

Steve hummed as Ogenos seemed very insistent on doing what he wanted. He might've gotten away with that attitude back where he lived because of his status, but things worked a bit differently here. Steve felt it was his moral obligation to explain that to him. "You're right. I could find another job. But it wouldn't be as easy. And right now, I kinda need this job..."

"You mean want, don't you?"

"No. Need. Jobs give you money." Steve gestured to the broom Ogenos held. "Money that let me buy that broom you're holding, as well as the clothes you're wearing right

now. It's also what lets me keep things in the house func-
tioning."

Ogenos grumbled. "I know how currency works."

Steve raised his hands defensively. "Sorry, didn't mean to
mock your intelligence. All I'm saying is that sometimes,
you have to do things you don't really wanna do and wear
clothes you would rather not wear. It's just how it is."
Ogenos huffed, seemingly bummed out by that fact.

"Ah, don't worry! It's not like jobs are bone-breaking or
spirit-shattering." He paused. "At least, mine isn't. In fact,
I'd say I'm very well off! I get paid a lot, the job itself is easy,
the people are nice, and the best part is I work the morning
shifts. So I have the evenings to myself!"

"Isn't the morning almost over?" Ogenos pointed out.

"Shoot!" He blurted, realizing he had spent a tad too long
explaining things to Ogenos. "Right, uh, I'll be back later,
Ogenos! You don't have to, but if you'd like, you can do all
the chores on that list I gave you last night. When I get
back, we'll go over proper etiquette!" Steve said, rushing the
words out of his mouth almost as fast as he rushed out the
door.

Steve was on the road instantly. However, after checking the time repeatedly, he knew he wasn't going to make it on time today.

"Man..." He sighed, a bit saddened that his perfect streak of being on time for five years straight would be broken. "Guess it happens to the best of us." He accepted, shifting his thoughts to Ogenos.

Steve didn't know much about the alien, but he did know two things. He was incredibly powerful, but he was also incredibly... depressed.

It was subtle. Quick glances wouldn't have been able to tell him that. But the more Steve observed and listened to Ogenos, the more it just became painfully obvious. In a way, it had almost mirrored him.

Thoughts invaded Steve's mind as he wondered what could drive such a being like Ogenos to sadness.

Was the strain of saving people really too much? Again, Steve had never lived that life, but he assumed after doing it for so long, you'd get used to it.

Maybe Ogenos lost someone close to him, and the failure of being unable to save them shattered his drive to continue being a hero? That was certainly a possibility, but who?

Ah, it wasn't any of his business. Steve's only concern was getting Ogenos accustomed to Tyran—something he'd be more than happy to do!

...After work, of course.

A short drive later, Steve found himself in a bustling part of the city.

He parked in an empty lot belonging to a building that shared the same red and yellow color schemes as his uniform. On top of the building was a large smiling burger resembling the one on his badge. Plastered on the front were the bold words 'Happy Burger.'

"Another day, another shift." He said with enthusiasm, making his way around the building to enter through the employees-only entrance in the back.

He stepped into the kitchen, and Immediately, the delicious smell of fries, burgers, and nuggets hit his nostrils. The place hadn't opened yet, which meant what he smelled now were the leftover aromas from last night.

"Well, if it isn't the man of the hour!" An older, familiar voice boomed from the left. Steve turned to see an equally familiar face wearing the same uniform as him.

"Bernard!" Steve waved with a smile.

Bernard returned the smile with his own, showing off his dangerously sharp teeth. Anyone else would be intimidated by such a sight, but Steve had grown used to it.

Bernard lumbered over, his bald head glimmering underneath the kitchen lights. "It's unlike you to be the last one here!" He softly patted Steve's back with a large, green hand.

Even though he was being gentle, Bernard nearly made Steve stumble forward. That was to be expected, considering he was an ogre. As far as ogres went, he was actually pretty short for their kind. Still, he towered over Steve, not that he minded.

"Sorry, sorry." Steve apologized, adjusting his badge. "Didn't get much sleep last night." He admitted.

Bernard stroked his black, curly beard. His eyes held a glint of concern in them, but he didn't voice it.

"Wait, you mean everyone else is here?" Steve asked, only now processing what Bernard said.

"Y-Yes." A more timid voice spoke out from behind.

It came from a smaller lady, who was just an inch shorter than Steve, and also wore the Happy Burger uniform. Her long black hair draped over both the uniform and her pink skin. "Are you okay, Mr. Gale?" The woman asked as her singular large gray eye blinked.

"What? What kind of question is that? And how many times do I have to say it, Kate? I'm your boss, not corporate. You can call me Steve!" He said that last part reassuringly, but that didn't keep Kate from stammering a response.

"R-Right. S-Sorry, sir."

Steve shook his head dismissively. "You're fine. Besides, of course I'm okay. Why wouldn't I be?"

"Well, it's just..." Kate looked everywhere *but* at Steve, unable to get her thoughts out.

That's when Bernard stepped around to be in Steve's view. "Not to press or anything, but I haven't seen you late for work in... well, years. Even after—" Bernard stopped himself. "Well, y'know. We already finished prep 'cause of how long ya took!"

Oh, so that's why Kate looks so worried. Wait, I wasn't that late, was I? Steve stared at Bernard absentmindedly, making him cross his arms.

"Everything alright?"

"O-Oh! Yeah, yeah. I promise I'm alright. Honest! I was just up late with my new roommate, is all."

"Roommate?!" A new, tomboyish voice called out, abruptly standing up from behind a metal rack. The figure hit their head on a set of pans that were hung up on the top of the rack, causing them to fall and clatter to the ground.

"Ooo." Steve winced. "You alright, Brie?"

Brie mumbled a "Yeah" in response as she rubbed her head, stepping around the rack to reveal herself. She was a... well, nobody knew what she was.

She was a humanoid of some kind, being slightly taller than Bernard. Paired with her tallness were two dark red horns that protruded from her forehead. Others would find the horns to be scary, but Steve found them comforting, oddly enough. Of course, he never said that to her.

"What do you mean 'new roommate?'" Brie questioned, gritting her sharp teeth.

Steve wasn't sure why that got such a strong reaction out of her, but he explained himself anyway. "I found a guy the other day completely unconscious, so I took him back to my place, and, well, now we're roomies! Neat, huh?"

A dark red blush appeared on Brie's cheeks, which was hard to spot as it blended in with her hellish red skin. "O-Oh." She raised a clawed hand, gently brushing aside her snow-white pigtailed-styled hair. "I see." Her usually confident voice held a tone of embarrassment that he would only hear from Kate, and her reddish-orange eyes averted from Steve's.

Before he could comment on Brie's sudden shyness, Bernard butted in. "Hold on. You mean you brought home some random dude you found knocked out on the streets?"

"Well, yeah. I couldn't just leave him there."

"So you thought taking some stranger back home with you was a smart decision as opposed to calling the local authorities?"

Steve paused, thinking of an excuse. "Look, I wasn't really thinking clearly, alright? I was tired, and it was night. Plus, even if I had called the police, there was no guarantee they would've found him before the Ragin' Bulls. Bringing him back home was the only way I could be certain he'd be alright." Bernard frowned but had an understanding look in his gaze. Steve knew he meant well and was only looking out for him. "And like I said, we're roommates now! Turns out, he's a pretty decent guy—Not from around here though, so I offered him to crash at my place 'til he can get back on his feet."

Bernard grumbled. "Just don't make that a habit, Steve."

"Oh, don't you worry so much! Look, if it makes you happy, that'll be the first and last time I do something like that." He patted the ogre's arm as reassurance. "Now then, what are we standing around for? It's almost time to open! Rev up those fryers and start those grills. We got customers to feed and happy burgers to make!"

Once the crew shifted in gear, hungry customers started showing up in droves. They piled in over one another, drawn by the scent of greasy fries and beefy burgers.

Steve and Brie worked the front counter together, taking orders and payments for them. Kate was on server duty, delivering food to customers who chose to eat inside. This left Bernard to man the kitchen all by himself.

With how many orders they get in a day, anyone would think one cook wouldn't be enough. Not only does Bernard make each order in a timely fashion, but even if a customer claims their order was wrong, he manages to whip them up a whole new one without slacking behind. He also keeps the kitchen clean at all times, even during rush hour. Steve isn't sure how he does it, but Bernard surpasses his expectations every single shift. Really, everyone does!

Kate, even with her difficulties in talking to people, puts in the effort and doesn't let that hinder her work. She might act shy from time to time, but when it really comes down to it, she can hold her own.

Brie has also surprised Steve a few times. She's the newest in the crew, having only worked with them for the past year and a half. Despite that, she proved herself a fast learner. With everything she's done thus far, there was no doubt in Steve's mind that she would come for his position in the near future... At least for now, he can enjoy their synchronized teamwork.

Everything went smoothly. At least, it did. "Hello, Stevie." Steve instantly knew who spoke, even when his eyes were glued to the monitor in front of him. He hesitantly peered up to see an unpleasant face: Maya. "Still selling burgers to pay the bills, I see? That's so like you." She snickered.

From the corner of his eye, he could see Brie scowling

at the elf. Maya's presence wasn't exactly new, so it was no mystery why everyone disliked her, even Kate. However, Brie's contempt for Maya started way before she dumped him. Why? He didn't know.

As much as he disliked Maya, this was a professional environment. She might've been his ex, but right now, she was a customer. As such, he couldn't have his employees scowling at her. He let Brie know this with a slight but noticeable shake of his head; she stopped scowling immediately.

He gave Maya his attention once again, offering her a polite, albeit forced, smile. "Welcome to Happy Burgers. Would you like to order something? Maybe for you and your boyfriend?" Steve abruptly paused, unsure why he felt the need to add that last sentence.

"Well, duh." Maya slammed a recently manicured hand on the desk.

"Why else would I come to such a sloppy place? I'd rather drop dead than eat at such a shoddy establishment. Especially if you're in it." She let out a tired sigh. "Honestly, I don't know why Sam loves Happy Burgers so much. It's such a waste of money."

Steve felt his brows curl in irritation. Maya wasn't saying all of this when they were together. In fact, she was the one saying Happy Burgers was the most enjoyable of all fast-food places. Such a snake.

"Oh, but he did say he'd treat me if I got him his favorite." Maya swooned, grabbing her face as she daydreamed about Samuel.

Steve wondered why Samuel wasn't with Maya at the moment, but he had a more important question to ask. "What would you like to order?"

Maya scoffed before pulling out her phone, tapping it a few times before ordering—or rather, demanding—her food. Steve didn't necessarily have a problem with her tone. His problem was what the hell she was ordering.

She ordered so much food, to the point where you could feed a small group of people and then offer them seconds! Sure, Samuel was a minotaur, but they didn't eat this much, did they?

Regardless, Maya had more than enough to pay for it, so the transaction was short. What was even shorter was the time it took for Bernard to cook it all. He'd really like to know what that ogre's secret was.

Within minutes, Steve handed the large bag full of greasy food to Maya. "Thank you for choosing Happy Burgers. Please, come again soon." He recited, though practically had to force himself to say the last part.

"Yeah, yeah." Maya grabbed the large bag, holding it with ease. She didn't even bother to give Steve so much as a glance as she stared at her phone, typing away to Samuel, most likely. "See ya." With that, she was gone.

Steve groaned, relieved that Maya finally left. Brie, on the other hand, let out a beastly growl. "How could you just let her speak to you like that?"

Steve always found it a bit puzzling that Brie was furious over the things Maya did to him. Then again, her being angry on his behalf made sense. They were friends, after all. Still, he couldn't let that affect how she performed at work. "It's fine, Brie. I mean, don't get me wrong, I don't like it either. But while I'm on the clock, she's a customer first and my ex second."

Brie seemed to understand, but was none too pleased about it. She made her displeasure known. "We could just deny her service."

"Yeah, we could. But I believe everyone deserves a chance to be happy, and if you want to be happy, there's no better place to be than at Happy Burgers!" *She's also filthy rich. I'll consider any dime I can squeeze out of that witch a win in my books.* But he wouldn't tell Brie that part.

"You're so considerate," Brie said with a laugh. Steve glanced at her, seeing she was looking down at her monitor with a small smile on her face. "That's so like you."

Steve would take her compliment to heart.

There was a brief pause in their conversation. Both allowed the ambient sounds of customers eating and beeping monitors to fill the silence.

Suddenly, the floodgates opened as a horde of fresh, hungry faces piled in. "Get ready, Brie. Looks like another wave."

Chapter 6

A DAY ON TYRAN

"And done." Ogenos checked off the next task on his list, only to see it was the last one.

It had been a long time since he did something he enjoyed. The chores might've been tedious, but at the same time, they were relaxing. So relaxing that the flow of time became nonexistent.

By the time Ogenos became aware of his surroundings, he found not even two hours had elapsed since he started. "Liar." He clicked in frustration, remembering Steve had said the chores would take all day, or at least until he returned from work, to complete.

"I suppose it can't be helped." What might've taken Steve the whole day only took Ogenos, at most, a couple of hours. His extra pair of arms really came in handy for a few of those tasks, something Steve obviously didn't account for.

He sat in the living room, reading an encyclopedia about the different types of tyrants and their ranks. If he was going to live here, it was imperative he learn as much as he could about the "dangerous" monsters.

And yes, he should've asked Steve if he could borrow the book before rummaging through his stuff. But no, he wasn't going to. Steve was lucky he hadn't decided to remodel the house.

Ogenos flipped through the pages of the encyclopedia, paying little to no mind to the blaring television ahead of him. It was stuck on a news channel, and even though Tyran's technology was primitive, Ogenos still struggled with it.

The two reporters, a male elf and a feathered humanoid female, talked about the recent on-goings in Valentina City. Again, he wasn't paying much attention to whatever they babbled on about—something about the sudden appearance and disappearance of portals was all he gathered from the first segment.

However, some keywords from the next segment made Ogenos look up from the book. They were reporting what had transpired in Valentine Mall yesterday, or rather, the mystery of what happened.

The sudden arrival of a B-Tier tyrant had the populace shaken, understandably so. However, the city got an even bigger shock when the hunters reported the tyrant was already dead by the time they arrived.

Many speculated an apex-class hunter dealt with the matter secretly. That was all Ogenos needed to hear to get a smug look in his eyes. "I knew apex-class suited me." He clicked happily, ignoring whatever else the reporters had to say.

Ogenos basked in his glory for a few extra moments before catching a glimpse of the mall from the news. It was a top-down view, so you couldn't really see it had been ruined, as the outside was mostly intact—not that Ogenos cared for the mall's condition.

Really, the sight of it gave him an idea. He had finished all the chores assigned to him, and Steve never said he couldn't go outside, so why not explore the city? It wouldn't hurt anyone, especially now that he had new clothes. No one would mistake him for a hunter.

After a brief deliberation, Ogenos tossed the encyclopedia behind him and headed for the door.

Before Ogenos knew it, he was strolling through the vibrant streets of Valentina.

The city contrasted heavily with the quiet and still house of Steve's. It bustled with activity and was full of life. Maybe a little too much life...

Every step he took, a car honked. Sometimes in the distance, sometimes right beside him. On top of that, he could never walk more than a few feet without nearly bumping into someone. Ogenos tried concentrating on walking to his destination, but he didn't have a destination. Every time he thought about going somewhere, the chatter of the people, young, old, women, and men, distracted him greatly.

When was the last time Ogenos walked in a metropolis like this? Probably centuries ago. The change of pace overwhelmed him more than he thought it would. The only solace he got was the warm rays of the sun shining down on him.

Still, the warm respite would only last for so long. He needed to excuse himself before he did something he'd regret.

He saw his opening and dipped into a nearby alley. The warm rays of the sun didn't reach the cool darkness here, but he could deal with a little cold air for a while.

Ogenos walked further into the alley. The sounds of chatting people and honking vehicles gradually faded.

The alley was awfully quiet, bringing an almost eerie quality to the environment. The eeriness shot up when the sounds of sobbing filled the air. Curiosity filled Ogenos as he wondered where the noise came from.

"The date's due. You know the rules. Time to pay up." A rough voice said alongside the obnoxious sobbing. Something about the voice was familiar, but Ogenos couldn't put his finger on it.

"P-Please!" The sobs turned into broken, stuttering words riddled with fear. "I know you said today was the last day, b-b-but I don't have all the money yet! I thought I w-would, but I don't! Please, I-I just need a little more time!"

A hard thump reverberated through the alley. "Did he ask if you ain't have the money? NO! He did not. SO PAY UP!" A more aggressive voice roared, inciting more cries from the sobbing person.

Ogenos followed the sounds of the commotion, turning the corner to see a small, green humanoid creature hugging the wall with tears streaming down its cheeks.

Standing over the little green man were three burly humanoids. The alley was dark, but Ogenos could still make out the figures' fur and horns. *I've seen these creatures before. What were they again? Oh, right. Minotaurs. What are they doing in an alley?* He wondered while staring at the scene unfolding before him.

From the looks of it, the three minotaurs were trying to extort money from the green man. Assuming such actions were frowned upon in this society, it'd made sense why they did it out of sight from the public.

Now that Ogenos thought about it, he probably shouldn't be witnessing this. The group hadn't noticed him yet, so he could just turn around. But he wanted to see how far the alley went.

He contemplated for a moment, concluding it shouldn't be a problem since he was just passing through.

Ogenos approached the group, intending to pass them. After getting close enough, the minotaurs became alerted by the sounds of his footsteps. Ogenos gave them a dismissive wave. "Do not mind me. I am just passing through," he announced, paying no heed to the green man who eyed him, silently screaming for help.

Just as he was about to pass, one of the minotaurs stood in his way. "Oh, but I think I will mind."

There was that familiar voice again, and this time paired with a familiar face. "Oh. I remember you. You're that minotaur from the mall." He half-remembered, not caring to recall his name.

Ogenos simply referring to the beast as 'that minotaur from the mall' seemed to strike a nerve, as their face scrunched up in what he assumed was anger. "No shit. Don't act like you forgot my name!"

"It wasn't exactly important enough to remember," Ogenos admitted honestly.

The minotaur gritted his teeth in anger as smoke huffed from his big nostrils. "Think you're funny, huh?" The other two minotaurs left the green man to stand beside the familiar minotaur, and that's when Ogenos noticed they were all wearing the same biker uniform. *Is this how gangs operate?*

Suddenly, the green man took this opportunity to flee and broke away from the group in a sprint. Ogenos pointed at the fleeing humanoid. "It would appear your victim is leaving."

"I'll deal with him later. Right now, I got bigger idiots to address." Ogenos lowered his finger, already finding the situation tiring. But it'd be rude to walk away when someone was talking, wouldn't it? "I can tell you're new, and I'm guessing your buddy Steve didn't bring you up to speed, so listen up, cunt. The name's Samuel Kage, leader of—"

"The Ragin' Bulls. Yes, I know all about you and your infamous gang of beast-men. And for the record, Steve is not my buddy. He is simply a helpful acquaintance. Nothing more, nothing less."

"That's cool and all, but I don't give a damn." Samuel pointed at Ogenos. "Listen, motherfucker. I own these streets, and by proxy, that means I own you too. So get that through your thick fuckin' skull before you lose it." He yelled, roughly pressing his finger against Ogenos's chest.

Ogenos thought about killing Samuel for the simple act of touching him. But then he'd have to do the same for Steve, and at the moment, he needed Steve alive. He pushed aside his anger, releasing an annoyed sigh before nonchalantly moving Samuel's finger away.

"The only person in existence that owns me is me, myself, and I. If you intend to keep breathing, you'd be wise to remember that."

Samuel's face contorted into a weird expression, and his mouth widened as far as it possibly could. The minotaur was clearly about to yell more profanities at Ogenos. "Babe! I got you your food!" A feminine voice called out through the alley before he could, coming from the same direction the green man ran away in.

Unlike Samuel, Ogenos recognized the smiling woman immediately. *Oh, it's that long-eared elf from before. What's her name again? Mayza...? No, no. Maybe Mayu? Ah! Maya!* ...Somewhat.

After seeing how angry Samuel got just because he couldn't remember his name, Ogenos did not want to make that mistake again. Not because he was afraid, but because those situations were quite bothersome to deal with and could easily be avoided if he just remembered a name, regardless of how insignificant it might've been to him.

Maya skipped towards the three minotaurs happily with a large bag in her hands. The bag had the same smiling burger face that was on Steve's badge. Did she get it from his workplace?

Ogenos stared at the bag intently, and by the time she reached the group, her smile faded. "Is that Steve's friend?

Why is he here?" She asked with a twinge of confusion and disgust in her voice. Wait, why the hell did she dislike him? He had yet to do anything to her!

Samuel looked back at Ogenos, and the two glared at each other for a few seconds. There was anger in the bull's eyes. It seemed like he wanted to keep this pointless discussion going, but didn't continue for some reason.

When the other bulls took a step towards Ogenos, Samuel held his hands out and whispered to them in a low tone that he could still hear. "No! Not in front of my girl."

Was that what he was worried about? Maya witnessing whatever was about to happen? She already knew he was the leader of the Ragin' Bulls, and most likely already knew what type of gang they were. Why hide the violence they commit? The reasoning was beyond Ogenos.

Either way, Samuel huffed again. "He was just leaving."

"Does that mean this conversation is over?"

A vein appeared on Samuel's forehead. "Yeah, yeah. What-ever. Just get out of here."

Ogenos clicked his mandibles together, emitting a low crackling noise that faintly resembled a chuckle. He stuffed his lower hands into his pockets and crossed his upper arms. Only then would he walk past the four, heading the same way Maya came from.

Once he got far enough from them, Ogenos exhaled a long

sigh. "That was exhausting."

"Perhaps I should've saved exploring for a different day," Ogenos said absentmindedly as he walked down the busy street. It wasn't as crowded as before, but that didn't make it any less packed.

As much as he didn't want to admit it, his encounter with those minotaurs was the most interesting thing that happened today.

Compared to the boredom he felt now, Samuel and his anger issues didn't sound so bad. Ogenos wouldn't mind a little drama because, even though Samuel was as annoying as they come, at least he made for great entertainment. Actually, he could go back and instigate... Maybe swipe his food and eat it in front of him? Ah, but he wasn't sure what Tyran-food would do to his insides.

On second thought, maybe it was best to head back to Steve's house. He'd probably be off from work soon, and Ogenos would rather not have his guide panic all because he wasn't at the house. Besides, it wasn't like there was anything else going on in this city.

"Alert, this is a code E emergency. I repeat, this is a code E emergency." An automated voice blared out from seemingly everywhere as alarms went off.

The suddenness of everything jolted Ogenos out of his bored state. To his surprise, he wasn't just hearing things, as the denizens around him all halted their activities, worried expressions stuck on their faces. "Citizens, please evacuate from the vicinity immediately. If evacuation is impossible, find shelter and arm yourselves." The intercoms abruptly shut off after the message. That set the inhabitants off, as they all started running like cattle in a slaughter.

If Ogenos did his research properly, then the announcement meant E-Tier tyrants were on their way. Those were the lowest-ranked monsters, so that meant they were pretty weak. Why was everyone fleeing as if an S-Tier tyrant was about to show? He guessed the fact they were tyrants was enough to strike fear in the populace.

In any case, he should follow their lead and run, shouldn't he?

Just as Ogenos thought that, the ground beneath him quaked and rumbled. Then, the streets ahead of him cracked and broke apart, giving way for creatures to crawl out of the newly formed hole.

Their fur had a gray and black color scheme, and they were quite small, shorter than the average person from the looks of it. Though, unlike the B-Tier tyrant, there were numerous of them. It looked like a pack... wait! They were! Ogenos recognized them! "Woles!" He cheered with clenched fists, happy he retained some information from that encyclopedia.

Woles were one of the many types of E-Tier tyrants, possessing the body and teeth of wolves but the head and claws of moles. He wasn't sure what a wolf or mole was, but if they were combined, that's apparently what a wole was. They were on the weaker end as far as E-Tier tyrants went, according to the encyclopedia. Still, Ogenos should abide by the norm and flee with the rest of the civilians.

He only got a single step away from the emerging woles before one of them lunged at him with surprising speed. As fast as they were, they were about as slow as a slug to him.

Ogenos reached a hand out and the wole violently slammed into his palm, resulting in a strange yelp. He closed his three fingers around the beast's neck and held it up. The wole struggled to break free, clawing at him desperately while growling ferociously. Its strikes didn't phase him in the slightest, but it was tearing up his shirt.

Not wanting his clothes to get more ruined than it already was, Ogenos tossed the wole into another, sending them both tumbling away. The rest of the woles did not like that, evident by them baring their fangs and growling at Ogenos.

Why were they so angry? He was simply protecting himself. Besides, it's not like he wanted to fight them. But every time he backed up, the woles moved in, intent on keeping him from escaping. Their fixation was both flattering and annoying.

"Fine, then." Ogenos took a stance, seeing as the woles weren't going to leave him alone. He could outrun them, but if his strength were not a norm, then his speed wouldn't be either. Facing them was his only option. It shouldn't look too out of place since they were only E-Tier tyrants. Even a non-hunter could take them down, according to the book.

Ogenos's eyes squinted as he dared the woles to make a move. And sure enough, one did. They went to attack from behind, leaping at Ogenos with a gaping salvia-filled mouth. He spun instantly, raising his leg to deliver a kick.

As his foot was en route to the wole's face, time slowed for Ogenos. *Hang on. The last time I attacked a tyrant, their insides splattered everywhere... I doubt a normal inferior could do that.* He worried how his attacks would fare against the woles. A mere flick completely obliterated a B-Tier, so he didn't want to imagine what his kick would do to an E-Tier.

Let's try this. Right before his kick connected, Ogenos lowered the power behind it as much as he possibly could. Even then, his kick resulted in a loud boom that echoed through the air, and the wole was sent flying into another building, crashing through its walls like a cannonball.

At least it didn't explode. Ogenos eyed the other woles and saw they weren't backing down, despite him having just defeated one of their own in a single attack. From his perspective, they were fighting a losing battle. Especially since he was attacking them with only a fraction of his power.

The fact he had to hold back felt uncanny to him. He only ever did so when sparring with his minions, and even then, it wasn't by this much. These tyrants were incredibly weak—maybe the whole planet was. But the woles couldn't see that... "How bothersome."

Another wole lunged at him, this time from the front. He sidestepped, grabbed it by the tail, then used its body to hit another wole that tried to bite his arm. The wole he struck careened into a city lamppost, creating an audible snap upon impact and splattering its blood everywhere.

The wole used as a weapon fell limp. Ogenos then realized its neck had snapped when he swung it.

After seeing this, the remaining woles decided attacking one by one in coordinated strikes was no longer the most viable method of attack, so they all attempted to gang up on Ogenos.

Ogenos continued using the dead wole in his hand as a weapon, clobbering the others with intense swings. Since he wasn't using his own fists, a few survived his attacks, albeit incredibly injured. Even then, they only got right back up just to attack him again.

A few minutes of this monotonous beat down ensued, and by the end of it, all the woles were either dead or unconscious. The body of the wole he used as a weapon was all battered and bruised, much to Ogenos's expectation.

He gave the body one last glance before tossing it, wiping his hand on his pants right after. "Great. Now I'll need to wash again."

Ogenos turned his attention to the surrounding environment, observing all the dead bodies belonging to the woles. Killing that crabor was one thing, since it was supposed to be strong. However, it brought him no satisfaction to kill such weak beasts like the woles. But it had to be done as an act of self-defense. He was sure—"Sweetie!"

The mature voice of an older woman rang out through the warm air, catching Ogenos off guard. He turned to see a humanoid rushing at him. They had the face and hair of a woman, but their eyes and the rest of their body were reptilian in nature.

Before Ogenos could say anything, the reptilian woman rushed past him, stopped, and bent over to pick up a smaller version of herself.

"Are you alright?! You're not hurt anywhere, are you??" The bigger woman said frantically, checking over the smaller woman like a nurturing parent.

He's seen this dynamic before. They must've been mother

and daughter—had to be. The child was a spitting image of the older woman, blue scales and all.

The daughter didn't look half as scared as the mother. Her big green eyes were sparkling with astonishment rather than fear.

"Mm-mm, I'm fine!" She happily declared, pointing a finger at Ogenos.

"Mr. Four Eyes kept me safe!" Though she said it innocently, Ogenos couldn't help but interpret the nickname as an insult... *Wait.* He took a step back in surprise.

That child... he didn't even know she was there. Was she really with him the whole time? Judging from the mother's concerned and relieved expression, the two got separated moments before the tyrants attacked. Ogenos found it hard to believe the daughter was right beside him during the whole thing. How did he not sense her presence?

As Ogenos ran the numerous possibilities through his mind, the mother gently grabbed one of his hands. "Thank you..." She smiled softly, a look of sincerity and gratefulness present in her eyes. Ogenos stared at the mother for a long moment, then suddenly disappeared from her view, leaving behind the indent of his feet in the ground.

While it looked like he had vanished into thin air, he actually jumped onto a nearby roof to hide himself.

"What was that?" He asked no one while staring at his

hand, which trembled uncontrollably.

It was the same hand the mother had grabbed. She hadn't done anything to it, at least from what he could see. All she did was grab it and give her genuine thanks. But why did it feel so... different?

Ogenos had been thanked countless times by his minions before—so many times, in fact, that he grew tired of their praise and appreciation. But this felt different—in a good way.

"So, this is what it felt like, isn't it, Genos?"

Chapter 7

A LITTLE HISTORY LESSON

Hours passed as Ogenos sat on the living room couch, impatiently tapping his foot on the carpet. Even with the emergency, it shouldn't have taken Steve this long to get back, should it?

"Maybe I should go look for him." He clicked, despite having no idea where Steve worked.

Right as the words left his mouth, the front door opened with a loud creak. A minute later, Steve walked in. "I'm back! Hope you kept yourself busy with those chores," he said with a smile.

Ogenos squinted at Steve, unsure if he was serious or not. "These chores didn't even keep me busy for half as long as you said they would."

Steve stopped, his face puzzled. "They didn't?" He spoke slowly, further emphasizing his confusion.

Ogenos confirmed by shaking his head. "I completed everything with plenty of daylight to spare. So, I took the initiative to explore the city by myself..." He rubbed his palms together as his mandibles clicked away in an odd rhythm. "Admittedly, it has been a while since I've surrounded myself in such urban environments. I didn't make much progress."

Steve chuckled. "Ah, don't worry about that. The city can be a bit overwhelming at times. Especially to newcomers. Trust me, I didn't get used to it right away, either. It comes with time."

That was... strange.

Ogenos could tell Steve knew his failed attempt to navigate the city alone embarrassed him. Usually, that would be enough reason for him to erase the human off the face of Tyran. But when Steve reassured him, he felt...relieved?

Ogenos shook the feeling away, remembering what happened during his exploration. "Oh, the city also came under attack by tyrants."

"Oh, that's n—" Steve paused. "What?!"

"You mean you didn't hear the evacuation orders? Or those obnoxiously loud sirens?"

"No!" Steve rushed over to the couch, swiped the remote, and turned on the TV.

With ease that made Ogenos envious, he expertly navigated to the news channel, showing a different pair of reporters. They chimed in on the tyrant attack that happened a few hours ago, revealing to Ogenos that it wasn't a widespread attack like he initially thought. Instead, the woles only attacked a section of the city.

That would explain why Steve was clueless about the attack. Still, it was surprising that he didn't at least hear the automated voice or those loud alarms. The city must've been enormous...

"Wow..." Steve murmured, his eyes practically glued to the screen.

The reporters would go on to say multiple civilians engaged the attacking tyrants, showing Ogenos wasn't the only one who fought them.

"I know they were just E-Tiers, but dang... this is the second attack in a week. What's going on?" Steve slumped down on the opposite end of the couch.

The reporters eventually finished discussing the tyrant attack and moved on to report other ongoings. Once they started talking about shoplifters and portals, Ogenos immediately lost interest.

He turned to Steve, a smug look on his face. "I was one of those civilians."

Steve sat up. "Y-You're not hurt, are you?!"

"Steve, I destroyed a B-Tier tyrant with a mere flick. What do you think cannon fodder like E-Tiers can do to me?"

There was a pause in the conversation. After giving each other blank stares, Steve laughed. "Right, right. I guess that was a dumb question."

Ogenos would refrain from agreeing, skipping straight to the point. "You told me I should be a hunter. At first, I was averse to the idea." He stared down at his palm. Even though they had long since split apart, it felt as though the mother's hand was still on him. "But... during that attack, I saved a woman's child. She thanked me with such sincerity. I've never been thanked like that before..." He'd purposefully leave out the part where he unintentionally protected the child, seeing as that wasn't all too important.

"What?" Steve said, raising a brow.

"What?" Ogenos repeated, looking at Steve.

"What do you mean?"

"What do you mean what do I mean?"

"You said you've never been thanked like that before?"

"That's correct."

"But you're a retired hero, aren't you?"

Again, there was another pause in the conversation. This time, Ogenos curled his eyes in confusion. "Retired hero?"

"Yeah! I mean, it was pretty obvious when you didn't hesitate to take down that tyrant to protect me. I don't know how old you are, but I find it hard to believe you've never been thanked for saving someone?"

Ogenos saw what was happening. He's not sure what clues led Steve to the assumption that he was some hero, but it was a far cry from the truth. "To be honest..." Ogenos looked away from Steve, thinking of another lie to tell him.

He obviously couldn't tell Steve the truth—If he knew even half the things Ogenos had done, he'd probably stop guiding him, which was something he couldn't afford currently. "...I was the one to coordinate efforts. I rarely ever got a chance to do hands-on work." He explained, staring at the television to avoid eye contact.

"Oh..." Steve seemed to realize his mistake in assuming Ogenos's past. However, there was audible confusion in his tone. "How are you so strong?"

"Genetics." Ogenos blurted. He wouldn't give Steve a chance to question his sudden answer. "You shouldn't assume anything about anyone. Especially someone you just met."

A thick and heavy weight of silence permeated through the living room. It was not Ogenos's intention to make the atmosphere awkward, but it seems his words had that unfortunate effect. Honestly, he wouldn't mind the lack of conversation, but the quietness of the usually chatty Steve was oddly unpleasant.

Ogenos sat there, uncertain what his next course of action should be. Speaking would resolve the awkward silence, but what would he even talk about? He already mentioned everything noteworthy that happened today. Perhaps asking what Steve did at his job would suffice?

Ogenos nodded to himself upon reaching that conclusion, then turned to Steve and opened his mouth. "Can I be honest with you about something?" Steve said abruptly, beating Ogenos to it.

The words he thought to utter died in his mouth, and instead of speaking, an awkward clicking noise emitted from his mandibles. It took a minute for Ogenos to process what Steve asked. "Are you implying you lied to me?" He grumbled in slight anger. His trust was placed in this human, so he wouldn't appreciate any deceit.

"No, I didn't lie to you about anything. I just... wanted to confess something." There was a genuine look on Steve's face. It was the kind of sincerity Ogenos had only seen in one other place.

"...Go on." He allowed.

Steve leaned back on the couch, exhaling a relieved sigh. Or was it an exhausted sigh? It sounded like a mixture of both. "That night, when I brought you home. Do you remember what I told you?"

"You told me your name was Steve Gale. Then asked if I felt anything. Then you proceeded to—"

"I mean, after all of that. When I told you why I dragged you home."

"You said you wanted to help me." Steve nodded. "And

that was true...but it wasn't the whole truth." He peered away from Ogenos, gluing his eyes to the ceiling. "To be honest with you, part of why I brought you home was because I thought you were a hunter. I figured that maybe if I got in your good graces, I could... I don't know. I guess partially live my dream."

"Your dream?"

Steve nodded, his lips curling into a soft smile. "I guess it's true that humans are inherently selfish." He sat up, staring ahead at the television.

Despite it still being on, Ogenos could hardly hear anything coming from it. The only thing he could hear clearly were Steve's words. "Y'know, it's funny. I always wanted to be a hunter. I wanted it so badly. More than anyone."

"So why didn't you become one?"

"It's not as easy as they make it look in the commercials. You gotta have something the Hunter Agency wants. Something that'll help you combat tyrants. Every hunter has a gimmick. Even the novice-class do. But me? I mean, look at me! I'm just..." He somberly stared down at the open palms of his hands, analyzing every square inch of his fingers. "Normal."

He chuckled, closing his palms. "I don't have some ultra-strong power. I don't belong to a wealthy family. Hell, I don't even have good genetics as far as humans go." Steve's fists clenched as he held his head down in either shame or embarrassment.

"I tried to become a hunter. I really did. But no matter what I did, no matter how hard I trained, they just continued saying I wasn't cut out for it." His tone slightly shifted to anger near the end, but after taking a deep breath, he seemed to return to his usual self, albeit a little melancholic. "Eventually, I had to give up. As much as my spirit wanted it, I couldn't keep putting so much strain on my body for results that would never get accepted. It was hard to accept I would never become a hunter. I felt like—"

"All that hard work amounted to nothing."

For the first time since Steve's confession started, he looked at Ogenos. His face was full of surprise. "Y-Yeah."

"Hmph." Ogenos clicked, looking down at his own palms. "I suppose we have that in common."

"You never got to accomplish your dreams, either?"

"No. Quite the opposite, actually. I acquired everything I could ever want in this life. Recognition, power, fame, glory. All of my desires were fulfilled. I truly won it all!" Ogenos stood, shouting the last part with triumph. Recounting his accomplishments brought a joyous feeling to him. One that quickly died. "But... my dream never brought me the one thing I sought." He slumped back down on the couch, making Steve bounce a bit. "Satisfaction." Ogenos rested his head on his hand, making another clicking noise—this one slow and monotonous.

Steve stared at him for a moment, then laughed.

His laughter spiked irritation within Ogenos. He allowed himself to be vulnerable, and Steve dared to laugh? Even when they were both in the same situation? "Taunting me, are you?" Ogenos clicked angrily.

"No, no. Sorry. I'm not laughing at you." Steve clarified. "I'm just laughing at how ironic this is."

"Ironic?"

"Yeah." Steve took his shoes off and curled himself up on the couch, still looking at Ogenos. "You accomplished your dreams, but you find yourself unhappy. I'm guessing that's what brought you here?" Ogenos nodded, inciting another chuckle from Steve. "Well, I was unable to accomplish my dreams, but I'm still happy."

Ogenos fumbled over his words, unable to express his confusion. "B-But you just went on a whole spiel about how you were unable to become a hunter! Aren't you depressed about that?" Steve laughed harder, and instead of angering Ogenos, he grew more confused.

It took a minute for the human to compose himself. Once he did, he offered Ogenos a more serious answer. "Well, yeah. I was for a while," Steve admitted, curling up on the couch further. "But I had to remind myself that the whole reason I wanted to become a hunter in the first place was to help people. And you know what? I realized I could do that without being a hunter." He shrugged his shoulders before leaning back. "After I came to that conclusion, I only really had two options: continue wallowing in my own self-pity or do something different with my life. And trust me, that first option is not fun."

Finally, Steve uncurled himself rather quickly, letting his feet slam into the floor to create an audible but muffled thunk. "I might not have gotten to live my dream life, not even a little. But that doesn't mean I'm unhappy with my current situation. The way I see it, as long as I get to help people, that's all I can really ask for."

"Help people..." Ogenos repeated, staring at the same hand the humanoid mother had grabbed. "You're a lot like my brother." He said absentmindedly, not catching the spark in Steve's eyes.

"I didn't know you had a brother," Steve exclaimed with excitement.

Ogenos jolted, realizing what he had revealed. It was too late to backpedal on his statement. "Yes... I did."

The excited and happy expression on Steve's face quickly morphed into a look of gloom. "What happened?" There was no malice or ill-intent in his tone. He sounded genuinely curious. Either way, Ogenos did not respond.

Ironically enough, his silence was received loud and clear by Steve. "S-Sorry. That was an insensitive thing to ask," He said awkwardly, rubbing the back of his neck as Ogenos remained silent. He didn't even so much as glance at Steve.

"Hey," Steve called out, a nervous smile sprawled across his face. "You said you didn't make much progress on exploring the city today, right? Why don't I take you with me to work tomorrow?"

That got a reaction out of Ogenos. "That's possible?"

"Sure it is! I'm the manager, so it should be fine. Plus, the others are really cool. I think you'd get along with them." He looked around the spotless living room. "I mean, it would beat staying here alone for hours, right?"

"Perhaps..." Ogenos clicked lowly.

"Then it's settled! You're coming with me tomorrow to see how Steve here makes the big bucks." He stood up with a groan and stretched. His joints made an uncomfortable popping noise, but Steve looked less in pain and more relieved the more they popped. "First things first, lemme grab a shower. Don't wanna ruin your hard work by dirtying the place." He finished stretching and sauntered elsewhere, leaving Ogenos alone.

Ogenos stared back at his hand, unable to forget the fleeting feeling of the mother who grabbed it. It was his first time doing an act that wasn't in service to himself. Even if it wasn't intentional, it felt euphoric. Doing simple chores that Steve assigned him was a nice change of pace, but this... This left him satisfied.

"I wonder if the agency needs more hunters..."

Chapter 8

MORE TYRANTS?

"These are your coworkers?" Ogenos asked while pressing his four hands onto the glass window of Happy Burgers.

"Yep," Steve confirmed with a smile. "Our crew is pretty small, all things considered. But we get the job done." He glanced at Ogenos, doing a double take. "Something wrong?"

Ogenos took his eyes off the four humanoids inside, staring back at Steve. He was caught off guard by Steve's question, as it meant he understood the mannerisms on his face well enough to tell what he'd been feeling. The two hadn't known each other very long, so Steve must've spent a considerable amount of time studying his face while they were together. The thought of which creeped him out immensely.

"Uh, Ogenos? You there?"

Ogenos snapped out of his thoughts, realizing he hadn't given Steve an answer and had been blankly staring at him the whole time.

He shook his head, returning his attention back to the

three inside, who seemed too busy to notice Steve and Ogenos watching them. "I just expected your coworkers to be like you." Even here, there was no lack of diversity. Now that he thought about it, he hadn't met a single human through Steve yet.

"Oh." Steve chuckled awkwardly. "No, we're not exactly the same. But they're all good people!"

Ogenos clicked his mandibles in an odd rhythm, pointing at someone through the window. "Who is the green one?"

"That's Bernard! Bernard Coleman. He's an ogre and the best cook this place has. Decent guy, I tell ya. Oh, just don't call him Bernie. He hates that name."

Ogenos made a mental note before shifting his finger to the next person, not bothering to ask what an ogre was. "And what about the human with the skin condition and deformed eye?"

"Her name's Katie Beenie. But we just call her Kate. And for the record, she's a cyclops, not a human. So everything about her is normal."

"Even the one eye?"

"Even the one eye."

In Ogenos's universe, only mindless beasts possess one eye. Sapient creatures with one eye either died out or evolved to have multiple. The reason for that was because their lack of perception never let them live very long. At least, that's how Bellows explained it.

"What about the red one?" He asked, quickly looking away from Katie.

"Oh, that's our newest employee! Well, maybe not exactly new. She's been here a while. Her name's Brie."

"Brie who?"

"I don't actually know her last name." Ogenos gave Steve a disappointing glare. "Hey, don't give me that look! She's a... special case." Steve scratched his chin. "Nobody knows her last name. We don't even know what she is." He looked away from Ogenos at Brie. "She looks like an oni to me."

"A what?"

"It's a type of demon, but demons don't exist," Steve clarified. "She might be an ogre subspecies, but I've never seen an ogre with horns before."

"Why don't you just ask?"

"We have. But even Brie doesn't know what she is." A disturbed look appeared on Steve's face. "We've asked about her past a couple of times before. But every time, the only thing she seems to recall is a ruined city underground."

Ogenos fully turned to Steve, clicking his mandibles in a confused manner. "A ruined city underground?"

"Yeah. I don't understand it either. I can only imagine she's been through a lot." Steve's tone was littered with sympathy... or was that empathy? Ogenos could never tell the difference.

Regardless, he turned back to the window, staring at Brie's figure more intently than before. She had a rather muscular build, but it didn't stand out much compared to Bernard's, aside from being more slim. Her eyes were a different story. Whereas everyone else had a white sclera, hers was pitch black, resembling the deepest voids of space.

Why is she so different?

"Alright, let's get inside. We're starting to look like creeps just staring at them." Steve chuckled.

Ogenos believed it was a bit too late to be worried about that now. They'd been outside for quite some time, and there was a camera attached to the building not too far from them.

Steve walked to the front of the establishment, taking out a jungle worth of keys from his pocket—all of which were attached to a large ring. "Usually, we all enter through the back door so we can unlock the front from the inside."

"Then why aren't we doing that?"

"Because the back door connects directly to the kitchen, and non-employees aren't allowed back there."

"Why not?"

"Health reasons. Now, where is the key to the front..." Steve focused, flipping through each key like a page to a book. The more he sifted through the keys, the louder they jingled. "I only ever use three of these. Why do we have so many?! Oh, here it is." His spike of agitation washed away the moment he found the key he was looking for. With an insert and a twist, a click rang out, and the door unlocked.

The moment Steve and Ogenos walked inside, Bernard was the first to greet them. "Well, look who's the last one here yet again. I see you brought a special guest with you today."

"The only reason I'm the last one again is because I was busy getting my special guest up. He's a heavy sleeper."

"False. I do not sleep heavily." Ogenos said defensively, crossing all four arms.

"Sure, man. Sure." Steve laughed. "Gang, this is the room-mate I told you about yesterday."

"My name is Ogenos Verum. You'd be wise to remember it." Ogenos expected a tiny amount of backlash from his semi-aggressive introduction. Instead, they seemed to disregard it entirely.

"He's pretty big..." Katie murmured, having to crank her head all the way back just to look at Ogenos.

Bernard boomed with laughter. "Big is an understatement! Never thought I'd see someone other than that Samuel fella give Brie a run for her money."

Bernard extended a large, rough-looking hand to Ogenos. "Name's Bernard. Nice to finally meetcha in person."

Ogenos looked at Bernard's hand, making a low clicking

noise. "Yes, I know who you are. Steve told me all about you three..." He continued staring at Bernard's hand, unsure what to do with it.

Before his staring grew too awkward, Steve interjected. "Sorry! He comes from one of those insectoid colonies underground. I haven't had the time to teach him every social cue. That's my bad," He explained, turning to Ogenos before murmuring. "This is the part where you shake his hand... gently."

Ogenos leaned over to Steve so he could murmur back. "What? Why would I do that?"

"It's a type of greeting. We call it a handshake."

"Your greeting sounds ridiculous."

"Just do it, please."

Ogenos stood up straight, going back to staring at Bernard's hand. He examined it briefly, then looked at his own. His mandibles emitted a low crackle as he shook Bernard's hand, gaining a toothy smile from the ogre.

"So, Steve, what convinced you to bring your roommate here?"

"Ogenos wanted to explore the city, so I figured it wouldn't hurt to bring him to work. That, and so he could meet you guys! It'd probably benefit him if he got to know other people." He finished with a light chuckle.

Ogenos wanted to facepalm himself for not thinking of

that idea. How foolish could he be to limit himself to one guide? The more help he acquired, the better suited he'd be in navigating Tyran.

Before Ogenos could beat himself up for his oversight, Steve abruptly stopped chuckling. His gaze locked with Bernard's, and he frowned. "I hope that isn't an issue...?"

Despite apparently being the manager, Steve showed a lack of dominance when engaging with his subordinates. He'd make for a horrible leader.

Luckily for him, his subordinates weren't the advantageous type. "Not at all! I mean, if you trust him enough to let him live with you, then I trust 'em too." Bernard crossed his arms. "Plus, I'm sure Kate and Brie don't mind."

Katie shook her head, holding her hands close to her chest. "I-I don't mind, Mr. Gale." She eyed up at Ogenos again. "Nice to meet you... Mr. Verum."

Ogenos couldn't help but click his mandibles happily. Her one eye might've been unsettling to look at, but her formality more than made up for it. *This one, I like.* He concluded with a nod.

"Kate, you don't have to be so formal with us," Steve claimed, only to have Ogenos raise a hand in response.

"Hang on. I quite like the formalities. She may continue."

Bernard laughed at the exchange, glancing behind himself at Brie. "What about you, Brie?" Despite his words being directly addressed to her, she didn't respond. This caused everyone to turn towards her.

Brie had been standing behind Bernard and Katie the whole time, and even though she was taller than them both, Ogenos hadn't realized she was staring directly at him until now. At first, he figured she was basking in his glorious presence, as everyone should. But the more he watched her, the more it seemed like she was stuck in a trance. No, trance wasn't quite right... There was fear in her eyes—like a prey staring down its natural predator.

"Uh... Brie?" Steve called out, immediately snapping Brie back to reality and breaking her fearful stare.

"Y-Yeah. I don't mind either..." she quickly responded, looking down bashfully.

Ogenos wanted to know what caused such a reaction. Was his figure that menacing? Normally, he'd consider it a compliment, but his goal was to appear average. Then again, she's the only one to look at him in such a way. Maybe he reminded her of someone? Either way, that wouldn't stop Ogenos from touching his face. Admittedly, Brie's stares made him self conscious suddenly.

Everyone but Ogenos easily brushed Brie's reaction aside.

"Well, you chose a good day to bring your roommate. I suspect things will get busy," Bernard said.

Steve perked up, raising a brow. "This isn't one of our busy days. What makes you say that?"

"Just a hunch." The ogre grinned.

"A hunch, huh? Yeah, alright." Steve said with some skepticism, but didn't completely brush him off. "If that's a hunch of yours, then we'll have to shift things into gear."

"The prep's already done. All we gotta do is open."

"Oh yeah, it is almost that time, isn't it?" Steve looked to Ogenos, which finally made him stop messing with his face. "Pay close attention, Ogenos. You're about to see how Happy Burgers gets things done!"

In the span of an hour, Ogenos learned two things. One, Steve and his crew made a good team. And two, Bernard's hunches were not to be taken lightly.

The building felt spacious moments ago. But now, people of all species were swarming the inside, and within no time, the place became packed. Ogenos managed to find a booth in the corner, situated next to a window that offered a semi-decent view of the outside urban scenery.

With how many people were coming in and out, he believed Steve's incredibly small team would get overwhelmed within minutes.

Time would show him just how incredibly wrong his assumption was. Not only did they not get overwhelmed, but as far as Ogenos could tell, they were giving out orders almost as fast as they were coming in, and this was all without the use of super speed. The key to their success had to be their perfect synchronization.

Their incredibly fast service aside, Ogenos wondered what made Happy Burgers so popular. Was the food really that good? It didn't look or smell all that appetizing to him—though that could've easily been because of how alien the food was. Then again, the most likely case was due to his lack of appetite. Ogenos had long since lost his need for sustenance, so it wasn't like food was important to him in the first place.

Perhaps the popularity of Happy Burgers would just be one of many things about Tyran that eluded his understanding. Content with that answer, Ogenos quietly observed the performance of Steve and his team.

Hours passed. How many? Ogenos was unsure. By the time he focused on his surroundings again, there were fewer people mingling around compared to earlier. The place was by no means empty, but now he could at least see to the front of the counter without standing up.

"Efficient. Effective." Ogenos commented, giving Steve and his crew praise. They may have been inferior lifeforms (Steve especially), but he had to admit, he underestimated their capabilities. "Perhaps they aren't as meager as we thought," He said, recalling Val's words in reference to creatures like Steve.

Oh, right... Val.

It has been some time since he left his old life behind. By now, the Malfadian Empire surely knew their leader had vanished. Maybe leaving so abruptly wasn't the smartest decision? Just thinking about how his sudden absence affected his empire...

No. He couldn't think about that anymore. The moment he used the transporter, he finalized his decision to leave everything behind. Everything he built. Everyone he knew. All of it. Whatever happened to the Malfadian Empire was no longer his concern.

Still, he could've left Val something. He was his most loyal servant, after all. Perhaps a note explaining his departure would've sufficed? He could only imagine how the Supreme General felt after—

Ogenos stopped, staring blankly at the window. *What was that?* He questioned, realizing he was worried about how someone else felt over his actions. He'd never been concerned about the feelings of others before, regardless of who they were. Why did he care now? He had only spent a few days on Tyran thus far. Had Steve already rubbed off on him?

Ogenos leaned back in his seat, clicking his mandibles

while letting out a soft grumble. Perhaps this was just how inferior lifeforms are. On the one hand, that was good, as it meant he was learning to be like them. On the other hand, if that's true, would that then make him inferior? The thought only made Ogenos grumble more.

He lazily turned his head to the window, then paused. Outside, a crowd of civilians dashed through the streets. All of them ran in the same direction, which was strange enough on its own, but what gave him pause were the terrified expressions on their faces—and the fact they were tripping over one another.

Ogenos slowly sat up, paying more attention to the scene unfolding outside. Faint screaming came from the fleeing populace, some of whom even abandoned their cars. He hadn't noticed it before because of the conversations from the other customers, not to mention the loud racket coming from the kitchen.

Everyone inside, aside from himself, was still oblivious to whatever was going on outside.

Ogenos got up from his seat, intending to approach Steve and alert him of the situation. However, the second he stood up, the whole building shook.

The customers yelped in surprise; some dropped their food. Those who were standing lost their balance and tumbled hard onto the marble floor. Steve also lost his balance, but was swiftly swooped off his feet by Brie, preventing him from falling.

As the ground rumbled, the center of the floor cracked and split open, reminding Ogenos of the times the tyrants appeared—it was always from underground. Within seconds, the ground burst open, allowing a pack of tyrants to spill out.

It was the woles again, except this time they had brown and red fur rather than grey. There were seven in total.

Ogenos clicked his mandibles in irritation. They weren't exceptionally dangerous, even to the likes of Steve. Unfortunately, that didn't stop the customers from panicking.

"Get behind me, Steve!" Brie ordered, putting him down and pushing him further to the back.

Her quick movements were enough to set off one wole. It pounced at her with its claws outstretched, and its razor-teeth-filled maw opened wide. Brie delivered a brutal uppercut to the wole, sending it flying backward with a spin. It crashed to the floor, instantly getting knocked unconscious.

"So that body isn't just for show," Ogenos commented, figuring Brie had the vessel of a fighter.

A sudden growl snapped him back to his surroundings. There was another wole, this time directly in front of him.

"You creatures are ruining my relaxation." The wole launched itself at Ogenos with a roar. He grabbed it by the neck with a lower hand, stopping it in its tracks. With his upper hands, he hammered the wole's head in with an overhead swing. Its body immediately went limp.

Ogenos shook the body around a little, unsure if the tyrant was dead or unconscious. *I held back significantly that time. Are my attacks still too much?*

"Protect the customers!" Steve yelled, breaking Ogenos's train of thought.

He looked over to see Bernard vaulting the front counter with a frying pan. The ogre rushed to a humanoid customer who was pinned to the ground by a wole. Without hesitation, Bernard violently smacked the wole across the face with his pan, making it stumble off the customer. From there, the two engaged in fierce combat.

"Stay here," Brie said to Steve before following Bernard's lead.

She hopped over the counter and sprinted to a wole about to attack three humans seated at a booth. On the other side of the building, a different wole was about to attack a family of humanoids seated in another booth. Seeing she wouldn't be fast enough to save both, let alone her initial target, Ogenos decided to step in.

He'd toss the wole in his hands into the wole about to attack the three humans. Upon collision, the conscious wole yelped in pain and rolled towards Brie, who grappled it to the ground.

Ogenos turned to the wole attacking the humanoid family, instantly intercepting it by grabbing its head and violently slamming it into the table, just mere seconds before it bit the father. The wole struggled ferociously to break free from his grasp, but it had no luck. Ogenos pressed its head further into the table, keeping its mouth from opening.

The frightened look on the family's faces worsened rather than eased up. *Maybe this is too close for comfort?* Ogenos lifted the tyrant up and away from the family.

He held it in the air with both upper hands, then slammed its back down onto his knee, emitting a nasty crack. When he felt the wole no longer moving, he let it slide down onto the floor.

Before he could observe the family's faces to gauge if he did a good job, a loud shriek came from his side. It was Katie.

She was hugging the wall, cornered by two woles who snarled at her aggressively. She wildly swung around a red tray in an attempt to scare off the tyrants, but it did not deter them.

They lunged for her, only to stop just shy of her feet—Ogenos had grabbed them by their tails. Before they could retaliate, he repeatedly smashed them into the floor. Each impact made a small crack, but Ogenos didn't stop until the woles became unresponsive. He let them go after seeing purple blood ooze from their skulls.

Despite her hyperventilation, Katie managed to choke out some words. "Y-You saved me..." Ogenos nodded, confirming that to be true... even though it was pretty obvious.

"Are you alright?" Ogenos heard Bernard ask from across the building. He glanced over, seeing him offer a hand to the downed customer with a wole corpse a few feet from him. After a quick look around, he saw everyone else tending to the frightened customers. All the woles must've been dealt with.

Ogenos turned back to Katie, extending a hand out to her. "Are you alright?"

Katie eyed his hand briefly. Her face somehow grew more pink than it already was. "Y-Yes." She gently took his hand. "Thank you." She said with the same level of sincerity as the reptilian mother. In return, that tingly feeling flooded his being once more.

Ogenos's mandibles clicked happily. "Helping others feels great," he concluded, forgetting Katie was standing right there, though she seemed to be in her own little world. He turned back to everyone else, only now noticing how damaged the inside of Happy Burgers looked. *Looks like I'm not done helping.*

Chapter 9

PROTECTOR

It did not surprise Ogenos when Happy Burgers closed shortly after the tyrant attack.

The customers inside during the incident were given a full refund on their meals for the inconvenience. After they left, Steve and his crew agreed to stay behind and clean up until their shifts ended.

Ogenos decided to help out since he was already there. For whatever reason, Katie took it upon herself to aid and teach him how to help with cleaning. Considering her awkward nature, he thought it best not to tell her Steve had already taught him everything.

The five of them cleaned up as much as they possibly could. For Ogenos, the cleanup was similar to the simple chores Steve had him do at the house. For everyone else, it was back-breaking labor. By the end of it, everyone but Ogenos was exhausted, sweaty, and slightly irritated.

Steve notified everyone it was time to go home. It was then Ogenos realized how dark it was outside, which surprised him since they hadn't finished cleaning everything. Despite that, nobody stayed a minute longer, leaving Ogenos and Steve alone.

"Are you done?" Ogenos questioned, watching Steve quietly organize some papers at an empty booth.

"Y-Yeah, yeah. Almost." He replied without taking his eyes off the papers.

"What is the importance of those flimsy papers? You've been sorting through them for ten minutes now."

"Well, we're probably gonna have to close Happy Burgers for a few days. Maybe a few weeks. I'll have to send an incident report to upper management and the Hunter Agency to receive any sort of compensation. Hey, if we're lucky, we might finally get those renovations I've been asking for."

"Hold on, the Hunter Agency provides currency?"

"Yeah..." Steve looked up from the papers. "Why do you sound so surprised by that?"

"I thought the disposal of tyrants was their only responsibility."

"It's their main responsibility. But they're also responsible for other stuff. For example, If I ran a shop and a tyrant were to destroy it, then I'd fill out one of these papers and send it to them. The next day, they'd help me replace all that was lost."

He'd set the papers aside before staring out the window.

"Though, we got pretty lucky this time around since it was just E-Tier tyrants. Still, that's strange."

"Strange that E-Tiers didn't destroy the whole building?"

"No. It's strange that all these tyrants are suddenly popping up in Valentina. Maybe it's just me, but something about that doesn't feel right."

"It is probably just a coincidence."

"Maybe." Steve sighed. "I just wish I was strong enough to take on at least E-Tiers, like Bernard and Brie."

Ogenos noticed Steve's sad facial expression. His guide being overcome with sorrow would do him no favors, especially if he wanted to be home in a timely fashion.

"In my experience, humans are objectively weak creatures. However, that doesn't stop them from accomplishing whatever it is they set their minds to. You shouldn't let your own weakness keep you down."

Steve glared at Ogenos with a meaningful look, his frown soon being replaced with a smile. "Y'know what? You're right! I don't need to be super strong or fight tyrants. I'm good at other things! Like managing." He boasted, picking up his papers and going right back to organizing them.

Ogenos raised a finger, about to correct Steve, but left it be. He actually meant Steve should continue doing whatever it was he wanted to do and ignore his weakness, not that his other strengths made up for that one weakness. But whatever—as long as Steve wasn't feeling gloomy anymore.

Minutes later, Steve and Ogenos stepped outside into the cool air. The city appeared much brighter than before, and the bustling of cars and echoes of people talking made it seem like tyrants hadn't appeared a few hours ago.

"This city moves fast," Ogenos mumbled as Steve whipped out his keys.

Right as he locked the front doors, a voice called out to them from behind. "Ah, don't tell me you're closing."

Ogenos turned to see Samuel walking up to them without a care in the world. *This man-beast is everywhere.* His four eyes narrowed in annoyance.

"Yeah, we are. Sorry." Steve answered. His tone seemed less apologetic and more apathetic.

"Oh, come on. You lot usually stay open for half an hour after closing time!"

If you want something from an establishment, why would you arrive half an hour after they're supposed to be closed? Ogenos wondered, not finding any reasoning behind Samuel's words.

Steve crossed his arms. "Sorry, but tyrants attacked the place earlier today. So I'm afraid there's nothing I can do about it."

"That so?" Samuel groaned. "Guess that explains the sirens I heard earlier." He stared up at the blue moon with hands resting on his hips.

Steve shook his head before moving away from Samuel. "Well, goodnight." He desperately tried to end the conversation then and there.

However, Samuel had other plans. "Hang on, where ya goin'?"

"Home."

"There's a worried customer right in front of you, and you're tryna leave?"

"Right now, I'm off the clock. Plus, I told you everything that happened. What more do I need to say?" Steve turned back to Samuel, unable to hide the annoyed look in his eyes.

Samuel paused, same as Ogenos. This was a new side of Steve they had yet to see, so both were caught off guard. Though, it didn't take long for Samuel to adopt a more aggressive stance. "I don't think I like your attitude, Stevie."

Steve's eyes widened in both surprise and anger, only for his brows to curl downward. "Oh, buzz off, you one-horned prick!" He yelled, further shocking Samuel. Though this time, his astonishment was replaced with fury.

"What did you just say?" Samuel stomped forward.

That simple act jolted the irritation right out of Steve. It was like he instantly remembered who he was talking to, quickly regretting his word choice. He took a step back, and his mouth moved rapidly despite no words coming out of it.

Before Steve could profusely apologize, Ogenos stepped in between him and Samuel, acting as a wall. "You heard him loud and clear. But in case your beastly ears are dysfunctional, here's the shortened version: buzz off." He repeated, causing Samuel's nostrils to flair up.

"You're really starting to annoy me, you know that?"

"Good. Maybe then you'll know exactly how I feel each time a syllable leaves your hideous maw."

Steve spazzed out a little before actively tugging at one of Ogenos's arms. "Gen, stop provoking him!"

"Better listen to your boytoy, Ogenos." Samuel laughed, making his nose ring flop around. "Stevie here knows who owns these streets. It's 'bout time you wisen up and learn as well, 'fore somethin' bad happens to ya." He smirked with crossed arms.

Steve gave Samuel a disgusted look, which somehow made Ogenos feel anger towards the minotaur. "Stop calling me that." He demanded, stepping in front of Ogenos with sudden bravery.

His abrupt change in attitude further infuriated Samuel, who uncrossed his arms and clenched his fists. "What did you say?"

Steve flinched, expressing minimal amounts of fear. However, he refused to back down. "I..." He cleared his throat and balled his fists, staring right back at Samuel. "I said stop calling me that!" He said louder with a defiant look in his eyes. Apparently, defiance was a trait every single human in existence possessed.

Like Ogenos in the past, it angered Samuel greatly. "Guess you've been hangin' around your buddy for a little too long." He reared back a fist, making Steve's face drop. "Lemme remind you what happens to those that step out of line!" With a roar, Samuel threw a heavy punch aimed directly at Steve's face. He moved so fast that Steve didn't even have time to shield himself.

Seconds before Samuel's punch connected, Ogenos caught it with one of his lower hands. His upper arms remained crossed while Steve trembled at the fist that was inches away from his face.

"So this is your strength as a leader? Laughable." Ogenos squeezed Samuel's fist lightly, eliciting a pained yelp from the minotaur. Samuel immediately fell to one knee, but Ogenos continued applying pressure to his fist. Samuel couldn't even pull away from him, though that didn't stop him from desperately trying.

It wasn't until Samuel let out another pained yell that Steve stepped in. "Okay, that's enough!" He cried out, suddenly showing concern for someone who was moments away from punching him right in the face.

Ogenos didn't understand Steve's concern, but he released Samuel, believing he had made his point clear. "Consider that a warning." He crossed all four arms as Samuel stood back up, holding his throbbing hand.

He glared at Steve and Ogenos with fury in his eyes. Despite his gaze being full of hostility, his lips were curled into a smile. He even laughed a little. "I guess your size isn't just for show after all." Samuel huffed. "This ain't over." He pointed to Steve and took a few steps back. He gave Ogenos one last look before departing, finally leaving the two alone.

Steve let out a huge sigh of relief before turning to Ogenos. "What was that?"

"What was what?"

"You riling him up. Why'd you go and do that?"

"You're the one who got him mad," Ogenos reminded, resting his lower hands on his hips. "Why were you so worried? Have you already forgotten what I did to that B-Tier tyrant?"

"Okay, sure. I might've gotten a little heated over the name-calling and lashed out, but that didn't mean I wanted you to get him even more angry! And no, I haven't forgotten about that—but just because you have power doesn't mean you can do whatever!" He explained in a slightly annoyed tone. He'd then sigh, pinching the bridge of his nose. "Sorry, sorry. I know you were just watching my back."

Ogenos looked at Steve weirdly, but after thinking about

it, he realized Steve was right. Why did he protect his guide? Sure, he needed him. But it wasn't like Steve would be useless if he got a little roughed up.

What puzzled Ogenos the most was his body's response. Normally, he thinks about what he's going to do before he does it. But when Samuel swung, he reacted automatically... He was even getting angry on Steve's behalf... *Am I growing attached to this human?*

...

No, that's absurd...

...Isn't it...?

"You said you wanted to live a normal life here, right?" Steve started, snapping Ogenos out of it. "Well, people don't usually go around provoking gang leaders, so keep that in mind for next time, alright?" He warned, looking back in Samuel's direction.

Ogenos couldn't allow Steve to say that. Not after seeing him stand up to Samuel like that. "What about you, then?"

"What?"

"You held your ground when he called you... what was it again?"

"...Stevie." He repeated, looking none too happy doing so.

"Right. The name bothered you quite a bit."

"It's what Maya called me. You know, back when we were still together." Steve inhaled deeply, staring off at the city streets. "I'll be honest. You kinda inspired me to."

"I did?"

"Yeah." Steve nodded, turning back to Ogenos. "I've never met anyone else who stood up to Samuel without so much as an ounce of fear. And I thought... if you can do it, why can't I?" He laughed, rubbing the back of his head. "Though, I guess I should've thought about how he'd react. Didn't think he'd actually try to punch me..."

"Then I suppose it was a good thing I saved you, no?"

Steve laughed some more. "Yeah. I suppose it was." He walked past Ogenos, heading towards his car. "Welp, we've been out here long enough. Come on, let's go home."

Chapter 10

REVENGE

"Alright, I'm off," Steve announced, garnering the attention of Ogenos, who sat on the couch in the living room.

Steve was already dressed for work, albeit sloppily. "I thought Happy Burgers was going to remain closed for the foreseeable future?" Ogenos questioned as Steve adjusted his uniform.

His confusion was warranted. After all, it hadn't even been a full day since the destruction of Happy Burgers' interior.

"Yeah, it is." Steve stopped fiddling with the uniform's badge, giving Ogenos his full attention.

"Then why are you leaving for work?"

"It's still up to us to clean up, y'know." He answered with a chuckle. "Besides, I still have to submit those papers." Ogenos stared at Steve blankly, grumbling quietly. "Oh, don't give me that look. I'll be back sooner than usual today, so we'll be able to explore more of the city when I get back. Until then, why don't you work on some more chores or something?"

Ogenos gave Steve a slow blink before standing up. "Very well." He walked over to the corner of the room where the broom and vacuum cleaner was.

"See? Knew I could count on ya. See you in a bit." He waved before taking off, leaving Ogenos to his devices.

On the road, Steve found himself dreading the near future of Happy Burgers. The attack from yesterday wouldn't be enough to put them out of business, fortunately. However, it would paint their establishment in a negative light. What are the odds people will want to order food from a place that was attacked by tyrants, despite it being in a city that is known for its lack of tyrant activity?

Speaking of tyrants, that was the third attack this week! What could be attracting them to Valentina City all of a sudden? Could it be the portal issue he's been hearing about on the news? That's a possibility, especially if another tyrant is causing the portals to appear.

Honestly, Steve just hoped the Hunter Agency did something, and soon. He didn't move to Valentina just to be under constant attack by tyrants!

Suddenly, a car peeled in front of Steve on the road, snapping him out of his thoughts. He slammed on the brakes as quickly as he could, causing his head to jerk forward as his car abruptly stopped.

It was broad daylight out, so there was no way the idiot in front of him didn't see his car. Plus, Steve had yet to drive onto a main road, so it wasn't like there were a lot of cars out.

...

At least, that's what Steve assumed. But upon taking a second glance at his surroundings, there were cars surrounding him at every angle.

A pit formed in his stomach when he realized the car that cut him off matched with all the others. Same model, same tinted windows, and same *blood-red* color. He knew exactly who he was dealing with.

"Shit."

The driver's door of the car in front of him opened, and out stepped a muscular minotaur wearing the same biker outfit as Samuel, but it wasn't him. Whether that was a good or bad thing was debatable.

The minotaur huffed; then he fumbled in his ripped leggings, taking out a cigar and a lighter.

Steve frantically looked around for help while the minotaur took his sweet time. To his utter horror, the vehicles had stopped him on the most isolated road in Tyran.

Just as the revelation dawned on him, heavy hooves clacked against the concrete road, growing louder and loud-

er as the minotaur approached with a lit cigar wedged between his lips.

Maybe the minotaur just wanted to ask Steve a few questions and then be on his merry way. As unlikely as that was,
it was the lie he told himself to get his body to stop trembling.

Steve rolled his window down before the guy even made
it to his car. Minotaurs were known for their short tempers,
especially the ones in the Ragin' Bulls, so he wanted to be
proactive and do everything in his power to make this inter-
action go as smoothly as possible. He even went so far as to
unlock his door, just in case.

The minotaur stopped once he reached the side door,
turning to face Steve. The only thing he could see was the
minotaur's chest. Then, after what felt like ages, the minotaur bent down—slowly. They placed one hand on the roof
of Steve's car while the other grabbed the cigar in their
mouth. The bull took a long drag of his cigar. He wasn't even
looking at Steve, but rather to the side.

His lack of communication was somehow worse than if he
had been making demands like Steve expected. At this point,
he couldn't even tell if everything was quiet. The pounding
beat of his heart was the only thing he could hear, and it was
starting to give him a headache.

The anticipation was killing him. Maybe the minotaur

knew this. Or maybe this was just routine to instill fear. Whatever the case, Steve felt as though he might succumb to a heart attack before anything else.

As if sensing Steve's concern, the minotaur finally took the cigar out of his mouth, exhaling the smoke right into his face. All Steve did in response was subtly wave off the smoke, trying his best not to cough in the bull's face.

"You Steve?" The minotaur asked, now looking at Steve with a rather bored expression.

Steve cleared his throat, swallowing the excess saliva that had formed in his mouth. "Y-Yes. I am," he answered confidently, trying his best to mask his fear. "Can I help you?"

The minotaur continued staring at Steve, only to give him a sly smirk. "Yeah, you can." He flicked the cigar at him.

Steve followed its trajectory, watching it land right on his lap. Unsure what the minotaur wanted him to do with it, he looked back up to ask but could not get any words out fast enough. The last thing he saw was a clenched fist; before he knew it, everything went dark.

Steve awoke to a throbbing soreness all over his face, which was further intensified by the bright lights of the... *Wait, where am I?* The suddenness of no longer being in his car woke him up faster, allowing his eyes to adjust to the brightness.

Around him were rows of empty racks and scattered crates. Some crates were open, revealing piles of various automatic weaponry haphazardly stacked on top of each other.

A warehouse? He recognized the layout of the building, though as far as warehouses went, it looked pretty abandoned.

There was an unpleasant smell in the air that made his face scrunch up. The smell came from numerous trash piles that looked to be all around the warehouse.

He went to cover his nose, only to find himself unable to move his arms. After some quick observations, Steve noticed he was rooted to a metal chair with his limbs wrapped in chains. He tried to wiggle his way out of his bindings, but all that did was give him an uncomfortable, almost painful sensation. Despite that, he didn't stop.

The more he tried to squirm out of his confines, the more the chains rattled.

"Ah, look who's awake." A voice said, startling Steve.

He doesn't know how he didn't notice until now, but the warehouse wasn't as abandoned as it appeared. Crawling all around the place were minotaurs in a biker uniform. The one who spoke stopped just a few feet from Steve, glaring down at him with a smug look. It was Samuel. "Had a good nap?"

Steve's throat felt dry, coarse, and itchy. The gravity of the situation finally weighed down on him. "W-What are you doing?!" He blurted, unable to keep his composure. Part of him already knew what Samuel was doing. The other part just wanted to hear it for itself.

"Nothing. Not yet, anyway." Samuel grabbed a sealed crate, pushing it to Steve so he could sit across from him. "I gotta admit, you've got quite the pair of balls on ya. I don't think a human has ever spoken to me like you did last night."

"So that's what this is about?" Steve's brows twitched in annoyance and fear. He had figured Samuel would be mad about that, but he didn't think he'd be *that* mad.

"Partly." Samuel cracked his knuckles. "Your little friend is hardheaded. That really gets on my nerves, y'know. Not to mention whenever he's around, you seem to get the idea that you can say whatever you want to me. That's no good."

"Listen, I'm sorry, alright? I had a long day, tyrants attacked, and... and I wasn't in my right mind! Okay?!" Steve scrambled for forgiveness, hoping he could ease things over before they got worse.

"Cool it," Samuel ordered, before clapping his hands. Then, a random minotaur came from behind, giving Samuel a soda can. He dismissed the minotaur with a slight wave of his hand. "Lucky for you, my girl ain't exactly done with you yet. Heh, gotta love elves and them wanting their fun."

Samuel cracked the can open with ease, taking a few heavy swigs. It was like the acidity didn't even bother him in the slightest. "Ah." He exhaled with a hefty burp. "Even if she was done with ya, I still got some use for you."

Steve perked up, oddly confused. "You do?"

"Of course. Your burger joint's the only one close. Killing you would be a hassle." Samuel admitted, taking one last chug of the soda. Once the can was empty, he crushed it effortlessly before tossing it away. It landed next to the other piles of trash littering the place.

"Besides, I could care less 'bout what some *human* had to say to me. All I need to do to put people like you back in line is break a few bones, after all." A shiver shot through Steve's spine. "Your friend, on the other hand, is a problem."

"O-Ogenos?" Steve spoke up, now fearing for his friend's well-being. "He's not dangerous to you or your gang!"

"Maybe not now. But he will be later." Samuel clenched his fist. "I know his type. He's got an inflated ego and thinks he can do whatever in this city. *My* city. That ain't gonna fly with me. Not today, not ever." Steve held in any comments regarding Samuel's hypocrisy, knowing now wasn't the best time to voice them.

His hypocrisy aside, he was just plain wrong about Ogenos. Sure, he was a little weird when it came to some things, but he was also very helpful. He had lots of power, but never used it to serve himself. If anything, Ogenos was the polar opposite of Samuel. "C-Come on Sam. You can't seriously be thinking about killing him..."

"I am. And I will. Gotta set an example, 'fore people start takin' his lead." Samuel shrugged. "Honestly, it's your fault for not keepin' him in line. I gave y'all plenty of chances to come correct, but like I said, he's hardheaded."

Steve's lips started trembling in fear of what Samuel would do to Ogenos. Sure, he was strong enough to take on a B-Tier tyrant, but Samuel and his crew were nothing to scoff at. He had to act fast and do what little he could to keep Ogenos out of harm's way. "You can't just keep killing people whenever you want!"

"Oh? And why not, Stevie?"

Steve gritted his teeth, ignoring the painful nickname. "The Hunter Agency will eventually get involved! You know that, right?"

"The Hunter Agency can't get involved with city affairs. Not unless the local authorities want 'em to." Samuel smirked mischievously. "And it just so happens I know the chief's daughter. Quite well, in fact."

At that, Steve raised a brow. It was no mystery that the Valentina City Police Department was noticeably lax when it came to crime involving the Ragin' Bulls. If Samuel were involved with the chieftain's daughter, it would definitely make a few of the puzzle pieces fit.

Still, there was one thing Steve didn't understand. The chieftain was the brother of the top-fourth apex hunter, so it was hard to imagine Samuel being able to blackmail the chieftain's daughter... unless he had very good blackmail.

"What blackmail do you have on her?"

"Blackmail? Who said I had any blackmail on her?"

"Isn't that how you bulls do things?"

"You could say that," Samuel huffed. "Sorry to disappoint any expectations you got, but I ain't got nothin' on her. Like I said, I just know her quite well." He grinned, staring intently at Steve.

Samuel wanted Steve to get what he was implying. His smug tone and the way he phrased everything made that obvious enough. But he couldn't figure it out for the life of him.

Then, suddenly, it hit him like an A-Tier tyrant. "You're two-timing Maya?!"

Samuel leaned back on the crate, his tail swaying contently. "So what if I am? It's not like you two are together anymore." Steve bit his tongue, holding back all the curses he wanted to pelt out at Samuel.

He's right. Maya and him were no longer a thing. They hadn't been for a while now. Despite that, he still couldn't believe Samuel would do something like that to her. Although Steve disliked Maya—hated even—if there was one positive thing he could say about her, she was incredibly faithful. Even when their relationship was practically in tatters, she *never* sought out a different partner. Not until she brutally dumped him anyway.

"Heh, looks like you've still got some feelings for her."

Samuel's statement caught Steve off guard. Then he suddenly felt hot all over. His face must've been beet red... Wow, it's been forever since he's gotten this mad on her behalf.

Steve quickly reeled himself in, wiping off any expression that might've shown his anger. He honestly shouldn't have been surprised that Samuel, of all people, did something as wicked as cheating on his lovers. If he was willing to extort the innocent, rob institutes, and kill people, why wouldn't he be unfaithful?

And anyway, this wasn't about Maya. Ogenos was the one in danger! "You're right. Maya is none of my business. Do whatever you want with her, but please, just leave Ogenos alone!"

Samuel chuckled. "Sorry, pal. But that option has long since passed. I'm gonna teach that four-eyed insect a lesson."

"H-How? It's not like he's just gonna entertain you and put himself in danger!"

"On his own? Probably not. But that's why you're here."

Another revelation hit Steve, this one worse than the last. The contortions on his face told Samuel he figured out his scheme. "Already got a message headed his way. Hope he's still at your humble abode. Otherwise, you'll be waitin' awhile." Steve held his head down, unable to believe any of this was happening.

"It's a shame you took a likin' to him. Or rather, it's a shame he took a liking to you." A sick chuckle escaped Samuel's lips. "Funny how he tried to hide it by claimin' you two weren't buddies. Y'alls friendship is so obvious."

Steve looked back up at Samuel, who was now standing with hands resting on his hips. "What?"

Samuel eyed Steve skeptically, only for his skepticism to be replaced with a devious grin. "You didn't know, huh? Well, guess I'm not surprised. You couldn't even tell when Maya had lost interest in you." He hopped off the crate and leaned in close to Steve, his grin widening the closer he got. "Ol' Genos has been usin' you."

"Liar..." Steve muttered. "Ogenos would never do that."

"Oh? But it's what he said." Samuel stepped back, cracking his neck. "See, me and him had a little chat a few days ago. Told me y'all weren't friends. In fact, I recall his exact words being: Steve is not my buddy. He is simply a helpful acquaintance. Nothing more, nothing less."

As much as Steve wanted to deny Samuel, Ogenos's

speech pattern was pretty unique. It'd be hard to make up something he said unless he actually said it.

Still, Steve had to believe in his heart that there was no way Ogenos would say something like that. "Bullshit!"

Samuel turned around, heading back to the crate. "Look, if you wanna live in denial about your homeboy, that's fine by me. Won't change nothin'. Either way, he'll come straight here, thinkin' he'll be able to bulldoze through my crew." He removed the crate's covering, digging through it before pulling out a large metal bat. "Then, when he least expects it, me and the boys'll flatten him and his ego to a pulp." He swung the bat a few times for emphasis; it gleamed in the light, reminding Steve it could be a tool for sport or an instrument of death. "Simply killin' him won't be enough. Nah. I'll humiliate him in front of his best bud, break every bone in his stupid body, and remind him who owns these streets. *Then* I'll kill him."

Samuel stopped swinging the bat after he noticed the ghastly expression stuck to Steve's face. "Don't worry. You'll have a front-row seat to the whole show. And when all's said and done, you can go back to flippin' burgers and seasoning fries." He laughed. "I mean, not like you got anything better to do." He continued laughing as he walked away elsewhere, finally leaving Steve alone.

Samuel's last comments seemed to reassure Steve that

he'd come out of this encounter alive. However, that was the very last thing on his mind. All he could think about was how Ogenos, a guy whose only want in life was to retire peacefully, was about to suffer a death undeserving of a hero. And it would be all Steve's fault...

He lowered his head in defeat, unable to escape his restraints. Why did he have to be so powerless? Why was he so weak?

If only he had the answers...

Chapter 11

THE RAGIN' BULLS

"In more recent news, the strange portals from earlier this week have been popping up much more frequently. The Hunter Agency is still unsure what is causing this phenomenon, but they've decided to dub the portals 'rifts.' Civilians have been advised to avoid these rifts should they see one appear." The news reporter stated, earning another tired grumble from Ogenos.

Ever since Steve left for work, he'd been scrolling through the channels, searching for anything interesting. Unfortunately, the only thing worth watching was the news, and to his dismay, they reported on the same portal nonsense.

"Nothing dangerous has come out of any rifts as of late, especially since they vanish almost as fast as they appear. However, with the recent influx of tyrants appearing in certain parts of Valentina City, the Hunter Agency has theorized these rifts are the result of an active A-Tier tyrant. Rest assured, the Hunter Agency has sent some of their best to investigate." Ogenos leaned back on the couch, using the news as white noise.

It'd be some time before Steve returned from cleaning his workplace; the house was already as clean as could be.

"Hm." Ogenos clicked, thinking about how to kill the time. Usually, his minions already had his schedule planned out, so he never had to waste time deciding what to do. Who would've thought the hardest part about free time was choosing how to spend it?

Just as the cogs in his brain began to turn, a loud shatter echoed through the quiet house. Ogenos sat up, turning his head to the source of the noise.

He'd heard the house make strange sounds before, but nothing like this. Odder yet, the shattering noise never happened again.

"Hm." Ogenos turned the TV off and stood up, walking out of the living room towards the front of the house.

Once he reached the front door, he was greeted by a broken window. There was a small hole in the center, implying something round had been thrown. But who would throw stuff at people's houses? That couldn't have been a custom Steve failed to inform him about, could it?

Ogenos peeked through the broken window. Pedestrians were out strolling on the sidewalks, going about their day-to-day lives with a carefree attitude.

Admittedly, it was a beautiful day out—which only made

it harder to believe someone would waste their time throwing stuff at Steve's house. Yet the proof was undeniable. What's worse, the culprit was long gone, assuming they weren't hiding amongst the civilians.

Ogenos stepped back, eliciting a loud crunch from underneath his feet. He glanced down, seeing he had overlooked some broken glass scattered across the floor. "Great." He mumbled, annoyed. It wasn't much, but the fact he had to clean up after putting away the broom and vacuum irked him mildly.

Ogenos's gaze absentmindedly shifted to a small white object on the ground. He blinked numerous times before realizing the object wasn't glass.

Upon further inspection, the object wasn't white. It had been wrapped in white paper, much to his confusion. He removed the paper, revealing the object to be a gray rock. Although it was a mere rock, it caught Ogenos's interest with its smooth texture and perfectly round shape. Without delay, he stuffed the rock in his pocket, planning to put it on display somewhere later.

After eyeing the crinkled paper a second time, Ogenos noticed black symbols scribbled across its front. The last time he saw symbols like that was on a wooden sign... *wait a minute.*

He straightened the paper out as best he could, finding

exactly what he expected: words. It was a written letter addressed to him. Even though he had no idea what the letters meant, he somehow understood the words perfectly.

When Ogenos finished reading the letter, he was left greatly displeased. "This is... false. Has to be," He told himself with furrowed eyes.

From what he gathered, the letter had been written by Samuel, which would explain the poor handwriting. He claimed to have kidnapped Steve because of Ogenos's 'blatant disrespect' and 'arrogant behavior,' ironically enough. The letter ended with instructions on what to do if he wanted to see Steve again. On the back of the paper was a terribly drawn map listing where he was to go.

Something equivalent to a small itch stuck to the back of Ogenos's mind. No matter how much he ignored it, the itch refused to go away. It was an unwanted plague on his being. Not to mention, it didn't help temper his fury.

Obviously, the itch stemmed from his growing anger. After all, how could he not be mad? His guide was stolen and might even be in danger. Yet, even with that knowledge, he couldn't understand *why* the itch felt so bad. He'd never gotten this worked up before, so why was it such a bother when Steve, of all people, was in danger? Worse case scenario, he could always find another guide...

Or maybe it was Samuel's brash attitude that got Ogenos

riled. From the moment he arrived in this world, Samuel has been the one pestering thorn poking at his nerves. Even when a display of physical dominance was asserted, he refused to yield. That was much like human behavior... but Samuel wasn't human. He was an arrogant beast.

Ogenos closed his eyes, thinking Samuel couldn't be that dumb to steal Steve. Then again, considering his previous actions, it wouldn't be unlike the minotaur.

It irritated him beyond comprehension that Samuel dared to interfere with his way of life. Part of him wanted to knock the minotaur down a few pegs. But in this situation, wouldn't contacting the authorities be the most civilian thing to do?

Ogenos thought about it, but honestly, he wanted to handle this himself. Once and for all. "Perhaps this once, I'll make an exception."

Steve shifted in his seat as best he could to keep his rear from getting sore. It was the only thing he could do.

Some of the minotaurs were kind enough to give him refreshments every now and then. Still, Steve wished Samuel gave him something to pass the time, like a book. Granted, he was far too busy being anxious and afraid to be any degree of bored.

He couldn't stop thinking about what Samuel and his gang would do to Ogenos. Worse, he couldn't stop blaming himself for it. The two hadn't known each other for long at all, but Steve liked to believe they were pretty close friends.

"Samuel." A voice boomed through the warehouse, its tone distinct and familiar. Steve sat up in his seat, being able to recognize the voice from anywhere. "You have annoyed me for the last time."

Steve and every bull in the warehouse turned their sights to an approaching four-eyed insectoid. Ogenos. He had entered from one of the warehouse's side entrances. The way he walked exuded annoyance, and there was a piece of paper in one of his lower hands.

"Ah, look who finally showed up," Samuel called from the upper levels of the warehouse, proceeding to walk down a flight of stairs. "Almost didn't think you'd come."

"Despite your poor directions, finding your dwelling wasn't hard once I knew where to look." Ogenos crumbled the paper in his hand, swiftly tossing it behind himself. "Now then, I hope you've made peace with your foolish misdeeds. Because there won't be a next time to think twice." He said in a serious tone, crossing all four of his arms.

Samuel stopped once he reached the bottom of the stairs, a look of bewilderment flashing across his face. Seconds later, he shook his head and laughed it off. "Wow, you're more arrogant than I thought."

"Being arrogant would imply I'm exaggerating my abilities. But I'm not. You and your colony of idiots are simply too dumb to understand when you're in the presence of a superior being."

Some of the nearby minotaurs huffed through their nostrils, clearly displeased with Ogenos's words. Samuel only frowned. "Y'know, Stevie over there was makin' me feel the slightest bit sorry for what's about to happen to you." He pointed, resulting in Ogenos looking over his shoulder to see Steve. "But now," He pulled out the metal bat that was strapped to his waist. "I'm gonna enjoy breaking you."

Samuel was clearly amping his threatening posture, but Ogenos paid him no mind and continued staring at Steve. "Ah, so he did snatch you up." He turned, walking past Samuel towards him. Steve started freaking out. He wanted to warn Ogenos and tell him to stop, but his throat felt too dry and closed up each time he tried.

"The enforcers of your home are quite incompetent. Fortunately for you, I am here." Ogenos assured, only to have two minotaurs step in front of him. His mandibles clicked in an irritated manner in response to the obstruction. He looked about ready to spit out an insult, only for the click of a gun to interrupt him.

Ogenos glanced around, and in that same instance, the minotaurs surrounded him; each one held a weapon of some kind. Most of the minotaurs had guns, while those who didn't carried melee weapons ranging from pipes, crowbars, brass knuckles, and even police batons.

"Right." Ogenos turned towards Samuel, who smirked. "I suppose dealing with you will have to come first."

Finally, after swallowing his saliva a few times, Steve managed to spit out some words. "Ogenos! Don't worry about me! Just get out of here!" He pleaded, unable to squirm out of his seat.

While Ogenos was surrounded, Steve could still see him through a small gap in between the minotaurs. He raised a hand towards Steve, gesturing for him to stop speaking. "This'll be but a moment," he said as if stating a fact.

As much as Steve didn't want to admit it, he could see where Samuel got the idea of calling Ogenos arrogant. There was no denying that he was strong. After all, not just anyone could defeat a B-Tier tyrant—let alone with a simple flick of the fingers. But he had to be letting that feat get to his head... How else could he not see how screwed he was?

Surrounding Ogenos were some of the most dangerous minotaurs in all of Valentina City.

Minotaurs, by default, were physically strong. But, considering the amount of crimes the Ragin' Bulls often committed, Steve wouldn't be surprised if that all toughened them further.

Then, there was the fact that the minotaurs brandished lethal weapons. At least when that B-Tier tyrant attacked, Ogenos was still wearing his armor. But now, he was in nothing but the clothes Steve bought him. Not to mention, he was outnumbered ten to one. Even if he could theoretically take on a handful of them, he couldn't possibly defend himself if they all jumped him.

Ogenos was at a clear disadvantage. It was so obvious... to everyone but himself.

"You're right. It'll only be a moment, lucky for you. But that won't make the pain any less intense." Samuel laughed, throwing the metal bat over his shoulder. "But hey, I'm a generous bull. You got any final words?"

Ogenos clicked his mandibles again, then dug into his pocket, pulling out... a rock? "A shame. I was going to put this on display somewhere. But I suppose in this way, it'll still be of some use."

Samuel sighed, shaking his head. "Really? A rock? I thought you'd at least pull out a weapon or something."

"For the likes of you, a weapon is unnecessary." Ogenos held the rock up, presenting it to the crowd. "This is the same rock you barbarians used to deliver that message. You broke one of the windows, which I will undoubtedly have to fix."

"Yeah, and? You gonna do something about it, or are you just gonna sit there and—" A loud bang resounded through the warehouse like a gunshot, interrupting Samuel. The next moment, a small hole appeared in his forehead, gushing out blood. Soon after, Samuel fell backward; his bat dropped to the floor, clattering against the ground.

A long, cold silence overtook the minotaurs. They couldn't understand what just happened—neither could Steve, but that was for a different reason.

The minotaurs didn't understand what happened because they didn't *see* what happened. Steve did, clear as day. Everything happened so fast. If he had blinked, he would've missed it.

Ogenos had flicked the rock from the palm of his hand, resulting in the loud banging noise that came before the hole in Samuel's head. With how fast the rock flew, it might as well have been shot from a gun. The velocity was more than enough to pierce through the bull's thick head, much to Steve's surprise.

"Beaten by a mere rock." Ogenos chuckled menacingly, clicking his mandibles together to create a haunting, crackling sound. "That's how insignificant you were."

The silence hung in the air for a few seconds longer before one of the minotaurs finally cried out, "BOSS!" Collectively, the rest of the minotaurs registered what they witnessed, and instead of growing afraid or even the slightest bit weary of Ogenos, they became furious. "KILL HIM!" another minotaur commanded, and all of the gang members armed with guns opened fire.

Steve instinctively threw himself and his chair to the floor, closing his eyes tightly and praying no strays hit him. His heart ached with how hard it was beating, or was that from him witnessing Samuel's death?

It was Steve's first time watching someone die in person; the fact it happened right in front of him made it worse. Sure, Samuel was a bad person, but he was still a person. Ogenos should've known to hold back...

Just as Steve's thoughts began to spiral out of control, they stopped upon realizing the gunshots had fallen silent. *Everything* fell silent. He gradually opened his eyes, being promptly greeted by a bloodbath.

The bodies of minotaurs were littered everywhere. Some had holes through them, others were horribly mangled, and quite a few of them weren't even in one piece. Guts and various other body parts were strewn across the warehouse. It was like Steve had entered a different plane of reality altogether.

At least, that's what he would've thought had Ogenos not been standing there in the middle of the carnage, holding a singular bullet. "As I thought. Your weapons are primitive."

He said while examining the bullet.

His clothes were littered with holes, implying he hadn't moved from his spot, which couldn't have been the case, considering the dead bodies.

Steve looked down at Ogenos's feet, seeing the broken weapons and scattered ammunition on the floor. The minotaurs obviously didn't break their own weapons, so what on Tyran happened? His eyes weren't closed for long, and it wasn't like time slowed down either.

Was Ogenos just so fast that he could kill an entire warehouse full of *minotaurs,* all within the span of *one* minute? No, he couldn't be. The only one who had the speed and power to pull something like that off was the number two apex-hunter. But... what else could explain the corpses?

A low clinging noise cut through the silence of the warehouse, snapping Steve out of his thoughts. Ogenos had dropped the bullet he was inspecting, now making his way towards him.

Steve frantically scrambled back, trying to get up and run. He didn't make much progress, as he failed to remember he was still tied securely to the chair.

Before he knew it, Ogenos grabbed ahold of his chair and propped him back up. Steve struggled for a short moment until Ogenos effortlessly removed his bindings in one swipe.

"There." He announced, taking a step back.

The scene before Steve was so gruesome and bizarre, he had completely forgotten Ogenos came to *save* him.

His fear and anxiety gradually washed away as he calmed down. However, with the wave of calmness came a surge of nausea. Before Steve could react, he hunched over and vomited all over the floor, prompting Ogenos to take a few more steps back.

It took a minute, but eventually, Steve got it all out of his system. To keep himself from hurling again, he ignored the metallic smell of fresh blood and focused on Ogenos's four eyes. "You... You killed them...?"

"All of them." Ogenos clicked, folding his lower hands together. "Now, Samuel won't be a problem anymore." Ogenos approached Steve nonchalantly, as if there was nothing wrong. With each step Ogenos took forward, Steve took the same amount backward. A confused look flared up on Ogenos's face.

Steve returned it with a disturbed gaze. "How could you do that? How could you kill them?"

Ogenos made an odd clicking noise with his mandibles before responding. "It was simple, really. Their bodies were frail, so I applied enough force to break them until they were lifeless."

"That's not what I meant!" Steve yelled, surprising himself. However, he couldn't afford to be lenient with Ogenos.

Not this time. "Why did you kill those people?!"

"Why? It was obvious why. They abducted you and attacked me."

"A-And?!"

"What do you mean and?"

"None of that gave you the right to just kill them!"

"How else was I supposed to save you??" His words caught Steve off guard. The way he phrased it sounded like he didn't know how to incapacitate an enemy. Before he could address that, Ogenos continued. "I don't understand why you're getting agitated. The Ragin' Bulls were a plague on the city, weren't they?"

"Yes! But they were still people with their own lives! What part of that don't you get? You're a retired hero, for Pete's sake!" Steve paused, remembering Samuel's words. "...But heroes don't use people..."

Ogenos stopped in his tracks, becoming as still as a statue. Though he didn't say anything, the surprised expression in his eyes told Steve enough. He didn't want to believe it, but...

"Ogenos, be honest with me," Steve muttered lowly, the silence amplifying his voice. "Were you just using me?"

Ogenos kept quiet as the two stared at one another. There was something he was keeping from Steve. Something big.

Before Steve could pry, Ogenos crackled a response. "I wasn't being entirely truthful to you when we first met,

Steve."

No shit! Steve wanted to scream out, but he held his tongue, allowing Ogenos to continue.

"I am not a traveler."

"Then what are you?" Steve asked impatiently.

"You once said you weren't sure what a conqueror was. I am a conqueror, or rather, I was. I seized riches, subjugated civilizations, and destroyed worlds. All in the name of my empire." Steve tried to process all the information given to him, but in doing so, he must've looked very confused, as Ogenos went to clarify. "In simpler terms, you could say that I'm a tyrant from another world."

Shortening his explanation of a conqueror to that statement brought clarity to Steve. Clarity that made him step back in fear.

Ogenos raised his upper hands, a poor attempt at calming Steve. "I came here to escape my old life. That part was no lie."

"And how am I supposed to believe that after you've been lying to me this whole time? For all I know, you're plotting to kill me! Maybe even conquer my planet!"

"If I wanted your planet, it'd already be mine. And if I wanted to kill you, you'd already be dead." Ogenos's blunt statement didn't make things better, but he had a point.

He'd been showing off his power from the start, and at this

point, Steve wasn't sure if there was a limit. Still, that didn't justify what he did. "Dead like these minotaurs?"

"Why do you keep bringing them up? If they were as bad as you say, then I did you and this city a favor by exterminating them."

Suddenly, the minotaurs that were kind to Steve flashed through his mind, causing him to yell once more. "Not everything is as simple as that, Ogenos!" His fear slowly dissipated, replenishing with anger and frustration. "There's a process to these types of things. Just because you have the power doesn't mean you can do whatever you want! Isn't that the whole reason you left your home?" He pointed out. Judging from the contortions on Ogenos's face, he hit the nail right on the head.

Steve rubbed his forehead, creating wrinkles. Until today, he'd never experienced such blatant ignorance. It was like Ogenos hadn't a clue on how reality worked and just expected things to work out in the end.

If he really wanted to abandon his old life, then he'd have to abandon his old habits and conform to Tyran's way of life. Even if Ogenos did all of that, nothing could excuse what he said earlier. Assuming any of it was true, he admitted to destroying whole planets... How many lives had he taken? More importantly, why? He said it was for his empire, but honestly, Steve guessed that was a lie. But if it was, what could the real reason be?

Actually, never mind. Steve shook his head, realizing asking such questions was pointless. Not only was it unlikely he'd ever get an answer, but whatever Ogenos did in his past was in the past. Nothing Steve had to say would change whatever Ogenos did. Besides, there were more important issues to worry about.

"I can't do this right now," Steve exhaled, mentally exhausted from...well, everything. "I'm going home. You... just... stay somewhere else for a day. Maybe two? I don't know... I'll talk to you when I'm ready." He said with a sad expression before turning and heading towards the exit.

As much as he wanted to report Ogenos, he couldn't deny the fact that he saved Valentina citizens from the clutches of the Ragin' Bulls. Plus, there was also the possibility that Ogenos really was trying to change. Steve had always been a firm believer in second chances. If he went back on that belief now, who was he?

With that said, he still needed a breather from Ogenos and his presence. Time was the only way he'd be able to sort any of this mess out. Assuming it could be sorted out in the first place...

Chapter 12

SPECIAL CONNECTIONS

Steve's reaction wasn't quite what Ogenos expected. He thought the eradication of the Ragin' Bulls would put a smile on the human's face—or at least the outcome of being saved! Instead, he walked out of the bloodied warehouse with his head hung low and an expression full of gloom.

Sure, Ogenos knew Steve wouldn't like it when he found out about his past. In hindsight, that was unavoidable. But that shouldn't have mattered anymore. If anything, Steve should've been grateful he handled the Ragin' Bulls, seeing as how the Hunter Agency wouldn't have.

"Perhaps he needs time to see what I did was a favor."

From what he could tell, Steve was in an emotional state at the current moment. Perhaps his kidnapping and sight of death sparked an intense, uncontrollable chemical reaction in his brain. That would be the only way to explain his unusual reaction.

"The things I do." Ogenos sighed.

Humans were something else. They're a race of violent

and aggressive apes, yet the moment bloodshed is spilled, some of them, like Steve, consider it an eternal shame.

Without another word, Ogenos turned and left through one of the other side entrances. Since Steve was no longer expecting him anytime soon, he could explore more of the sprawling metropolis at his leisure.

Some hours had passed since Ogenos started his venture through the city. An orange-colored sky stretched across the endless horizon, signaling the coming of night.

He took in the different sights and sounds much easier than before, proving to himself that he was growing accustomed to Tyran.

His sense of pride and accomplishment gradually waned, shifting to an uncomfortable feeling. He had no idea what it was, but it made him feel empty. "What is this?" he said blankly, staring at his hand.

Throughout his entire six-hundred and twenty-two years of living, he'd only experienced this sensation once before, but the circumstances were vastly different back then. So why was he feeling it again? Why now?

"O-Ogenos, right?" A voice asked, coming from behind.

He turned, seeing the same red-skinned woman from yesterday. "I remember you. You're Brie." He turned to face her, seeing she still wore that atrocious uniform. "Odd seeing you here."

"Y-Yeah," she responded awkwardly, not looking him in the eyes.

They stood there on the sidewalk in silence. Well, as silent as it could get with the many pedestrians passing by in every direction. Even when it grew dark, the city never had a shortage of people.

Eventually, it dawned on Ogenos that it should've been impossible for Brie to find him in such a vast, populated urban environment. Had it not been for her suspicious body language, he would've chalked it up to a coincidence.

However, before he could touch on that, she spoke up. "What happened to you?"

Ogenos gave her a confused look before she gestured down to his clothes, which were still riddled with bullet holes. He had completely forgotten to change his attire before taking his stroll. At least now he knew why some people from earlier gave him weird looks.

"I was in a situation. That situation has been handled." He answered, giving his clothes a quick look over before returning his gaze to Brie.

"Doesn't look handled to me," Brie said with a blank face, still staring at his ruined clothes.

Ogenos furrowed his eyes in slight irritation. "I assume you have something better to do than to engage in small talk with me, yes?"

"What's your deal?" She asked, finally looking him in the eyes with a surge of confidence that came from seemingly nowhere.

"What?" He clicked in confusion.

"S-Sorry. That came out wrong." She cleared her throat. "I just mean, why do you seem so different from everyone?"

Ogenos tilted his head as his mandibles clicked together softly. "Different how?"

"Don't take any offense when I say this, but I've met in-sect-folk before, and none of them were as blunt as you. Plus, you speak weirdly..."

"Offense taken." He grumbled, crossing all four of his arms.

"S-Sorry. You would think after working the front for so long, I'd get better at talking to people." She chuckled, making fun of her own awkwardness.

Was making fun of one's own faults really that comforting? The idea was strange. Though, maybe in practice, it wasn't all that weird.

"I assume you stopped me to practice your social skills?" He guessed, only for Brie to start laughing.

"What? No. I'm not that awkward." She quickly composed

herself, gaining a serious expression. "Thing is, Mr. G—" She paused. "Steve didn't come into work today."

"And that's strange how?"

"He's never missed a day of work. Ever. He always schedules his days off if he's gonna be busy. Even then, he'd at least notify us ahead of time..." Her gaze shifted from Ogenos to the pavement. There was a sad look in her eyes.

The moment he spotted it, she quickly returned eye contact with him, the sorrowful look now being replaced with subtle suspicion. "You're his roommate. Did something happen?" Although she phrased it as a question, she was clearly accusing him as the culprit. It didn't help that she eyed him intensely.

"You seem very concerned about Steve. What exactly is your relationship with him?"

"Relationship?" Brie blurted, and her face somehow turned redder. "W-We're just colleagues. Scratch that, really good friends." She answered with a slight stutter, clearing her throat again before regaining her posture. "As a good friend, I'm allowed to be concerned for his well-being. Now answer the question." She demanded, stepping up to Ogenos.

His anger spiked for a moment. He had yet to get used to an inferior speaking to him in such a way, but he had to remind himself that this was a common reaction from an agitated person. Besides, if Steve disliked Ogenos for killing Samuel, then it wasn't hard to imagine he'd hate him if he so much as laid a finger on Brie.

"Steve is fine. He failed to show up to work because the Ragin' Bulls abducted him while he was en route, I'm sure." He said casually.

Meanwhile, Brie's eyes opened to the size of saucers. "WHAT?!" Her yell caught the attention of passersby, much to Ogenos's dissatisfaction.

"Must you be so loud? I already told you the situation was handled." Brie looked at Ogenos's tattered clothes, appearing to put two and two together.

She got closer to his face, sporting a terribly worried look. "Where is he now?"

"Last we talked, he said he was heading home and told me to—" Before Ogenos could finish his sentence, Brie turned on her heels and bolted in the opposite direction, abruptly ending the conversation.

Once again, Ogenos was left confused.

Chapter 13

KNOCK, KNOCK

Daylight waned as the hours ticked closer to evening, and all the while, Steve sat in his living room, surrounded by nothing but silence.

He had yet to eat anything other than those snacks the minotaurs gave him. Despite this, his appetite was non-existent—not that it mattered. He couldn't even think about eating. Every time he thought about doing something, like getting his car back, Ogenos popped into his mind like an unwanted zit.

Steve couldn't stop thinking about how he lied to him. Sure, maybe that was on him. The two hadn't known each other for even a week, and on top of that, he was alien—completely foreign to any thoughts and ideas Steve considered moral and right.

Well, maybe not completely foreign. Ogenos obviously knew his deeds would bother Steve, which is why he refrained from telling him the truth. Though, that only made the situation worse.

Any normal person would take this as a sign to cut Ogenos off and let life handle it. Steve considered going down that road, but part of him feared what would happen if nobody attended to Ogenos. The extent of his power far exceeded what Steve originally thought, so for all he knew, not even the Hunter Agency could stop Ogenos if he chose to destroy Tyran.

Then again, if Ogenos wanted that, he would've already done it. He said so himself, and Steve fully believed him when it came to that. Ogenos also mentioned something about an empire... If he wanted to take over Tyran, he would've brought his legion, wouldn't he? The fact that he didn't had to mean something.

Maybe he really did want to change?

Still, he couldn't get over what he did was wrong. Even though Samuel was the one to cross the line, Ogenos *slaughtered* those minotaurs. But at the end of the day, he only did so to protect Steve...

"Dammit!" Steve grunted in frustration, unable to think straight. He turned on the TV in hopes whatever was on would distract him.

"This just in: the notorious gang known as the Ragin' Bulls have been massacred!" Steve froze with widened eyes, dropping both the remote and his jaw. "Earlier today, citizens reported hearing gunshots in the Southside outskirts of Valentina. Authorities investigated, discovering a small warehouse previously thought to be under renovation. What they found inside was a graveyard."

The bottom right of the channel displayed images from inside the warehouse. They were heavily blurred, so nobody could get a clear visual of what exactly was being shown. However, with how red everything was, and the fact Steve had been there a short while ago, he knew exactly what they were showing.

"The VCPD were able to identify a few of the corpses, confirming them to be members of the Ragin' Bulls. It is speculated that this warehouse was their hideout. Police are still investigating who could've been behind this slaughter, but as of now, no clues as to who the culprit could be were left behind. One thing is for certain, though: residents of Valentina City can rest well knowing the Ragin' Bulls won't be causing any more trouble."

"Shit!" Steve cursed instinctively, realizing Ogenos killing Samuel had caused a domino effect.

He had forgotten until now that Samuel admitted to being involved with the police chieftain's daughter. At the time, he wasn't sure how true that was. But after watching the news, he was fully convinced.

Finding the Ragin' Bull's hideout after years of evading authorities *and* being able to identify some of their members on the same day—especially after what Ogenos did to them? Not a coincidence.

Then again, it wasn't like Samuel or any of his goons ever tried to hide their faces. Now that Steve thought about it, maybe it was just because of complete negligence that the police hadn't caught the Ragin' Bulls before... unless Samuel and the chieftain's daughter had always been a thing? But then that would mean he was always two-timing Maya, right?

Wait, no! That's not what was important! Samuel obviously wasn't lying about his relations, and with that being the case, it was only a matter of time before the police did everything in their power to find the one responsible, that being Ogenos. Worst-case scenario, the Hunter Agency might get involved. And if that happens...

...

Steve let out a deep sigh before shaking his head. He couldn't believe he actually felt concerned for Ogenos's safety, even after everything that's happened. Even if the police went looking and the Hunter Agency got involved, he was sure Ogenos would be just fine. If anything, he should've been concerned for himself.

There shouldn't be too much to worry about, as he was ninety percent positive there weren't any active cameras in the warehouse. Besides, if anyone would be a suspect, it'd probably be Maya... poor Maya.

Suddenly, a knock echoed through the house. *Two knocks.*

Steve perked up, turning towards the knocking noise. He knew it came from his front door, judging from the direction the sound echoed from. What he didn't know was who that could possibly be. There was no way Ogenos actually came back to the house after what he told him, right?

...Guess there was only one way to find out.

He made his way to the front door. Luckily, he didn't have to address the broken glass on the floor, as he already cleaned it up the moment he got home. That, and he also covered his broken window with an excessive amount of duct tape. It was the best he could do before he could get someone out here to fix it.

Without wasting another second, Steve unlocked his door and threw it open. Whoever it was, he had intended to tell them he wasn't feeling alright and that they should come back another time. However, the moment he saw the figure, the words died in his throat.

He didn't recognize the person at his door at all.

The figure's appearance was eerily similar to Ogenos, but there were a few crucial differences.

Where Ogenos had blue eyes and purple skin, this person had purple eyes and hot-pink skin. They were clad in ceremonial armor, like the one Ogenos wore when Steve first met him. Perhaps the biggest difference between the two was that this entity had extremely long hair that flowed upward outside of Steve's view. It was as though gravity had no hold over it.

Before Steve could murmur any words, the figure stepped inside without his permission, forcing him to back up.

He cursed himself for not slamming the door in the dude's face. In hindsight, he should've peeped through the other unbroken window instead of just opening the door. Even if his neighborhood was a safe one, he shouldn't have been so careless. What was he thinking?

Suddenly, the figure clicked their mandibles together rapidly while staring at Steve with an intense glare. Their mannerisms came off as hostile, but they didn't make any directly aggressive moves.

Soon, Steve realized what the rapid clicking noises were. The figure was speaking to him, though in a language he couldn't even begin to understand. Unsure what to do, he slowly stepped away from the figure until his back hugged the wall.

After a second, the figure made a loud hissing noise, then looked at their gauntlet. They began typing on the gauntlet, which actually turned out to be a datapad of some kind. Their armor turned out to be much more advanced than Steve initially thought.

After they were finished, they aimed their gauntlet at him. He looked away and closed his eyes, expecting the worst. A loud humming noise filled his ears. Aside from that, nothing else happened.

He hesitantly looked back at the figure, seeing them now aim the gauntlet at themselves. A blue light projected from the gauntlet, washing over their body while making that same humming noise.

Seconds later, the figure clicked their mandibles together again. Only this time, Steve understood them. "Of course, the furless apes exist in other realms. Just our luck."

"I-I can understand you!"

The figure looked at Steve. "Ah, good. The universal translator works in other universes. That'll make things easier." They folded all four arms behind themselves, now speaking in an elegant tone. "What have you done with our Sir Overlord?"

"Your sir what?" The figure squinted their eyes at Steve, resulting in him taking a big, cartoonish gulp.

"There's no use in playing dumb. This place has our almighty leader's energy signature riddled everywhere. Yet, I do not sense his presence nearby. You've done something with him."

The figure was speaking nothing but straight nonsense, as far as Steve was concerned. However, he had a feeling he knew exactly *who* they were talking about. If the similar appearance wasn't a dead giveaway, the mention of an 'almighty' leader was. "Y-You're talking about Ogenos, aren't you?"

The figure got up in Steve's face, clicking aggressively. "Lower lifeforms such as yourself will address him as Sir Overlord. Nothing else." They threatened, to which Steve simply nodded out of fear. "Now, I'll ask one last time. What have you done with him?"

"I haven't done anything!" Steve said defensively. "I don't know where he is, alright? We both went our separate ways earlier!"

The figure remained in Steve's face for an uncomfortably long time before finally pulling away. "Don't feel like talking, do you? That's fine. There are other ways to make you speak."

"W-Wait, you got it all—" Steve went to explain himself, only to fall silent when his body wouldn't move the way he wanted. It was like an invisible force kept him in place. No matter how hard he tried, his limbs wouldn't budge.

"You'll tell me where Sir Overlord is. One way or anoth—" The figure paused; their four eyes looked to the side, eyeing the front door.

In an instant, the figure moved to the side with tremendous speed. Whatever force was holding Steve also jerked him to the side, throwing him against the wall.

Seconds after, Brie came crashing through the front door, punching the wall Steve and the figure stood in front of mere moments ago. Her strike caused a deep crack to spread throughout the wall.

Steve knew Brie was strong, but he didn't think she was *that* strong. More importantly, why was she here? Considering all the times he hosted special events at his place, it wasn't strange that she knew where he lived. But she rarely visited on her own accord.

"Brie? What are you doing here??" Steve blurted, watching her lower into an offensive stance with clenched fists. Even when she was hunched over, she still towered over him and the figure.

"You didn't show up for work. We all got worried..." Brie answered, not taking her eyes off the figure.

Steve frowned as the guilt pelted his conscience like a hailstorm. He never called the others after what happened at the warehouse. Come to think of it, did he even take his phone off the charger this morning?

"Oh... That's..."

"No need to explain." Brie stopped him. "Ogenos told me everything."

Casually saying his name got the figure to click their mandibles aggressively once again. "Even in other universes, inferior lifeforms continue to be disrespectful to those superior." Their angered expression suddenly eased up. "But this one shows potential." Unlike with Steve, the figure seemed to calm down almost as quickly as they got riled up. "Tell me, Red One, where is Sir Overlord?"

"Sir who?"

The figure shook their head, irritated.

"They're talking about Ogenos!" Steve clarified.

"Why would I tell this chump where he is? First of all, let go of Mr. Gale!" Brie shouted, barring her sharp teeth.

"A lower lifeform dares to make demands of me? How bold."

"Keep talkin' hotshot. Who're you supposed to be anyway?"

"I am Val Biox. Supreme General of the Malfadian Empire and humble servant of our Sir Overlord."

"Servant? Ogenos has servants?" Immediately after speaking his name, Brie started gagging on nothing.

She fell to one knee, gasping for air. After a few desperate breaths, she grasped at her neck, attempting to claw at whatever was restricting her airflow, but nothing was there.

"Brie!" Steve called out in concern, though there was nothing he could do as his body still refused to move the way he wanted.

"To regard our Sir Overlord with such casualness is to

invoke death. However, I have need for the both of you." Val stated, turning to Steve.

Soon enough, Steve started gagging for air. Val did nothing but stand there, and yet it felt like something wrapped around his neck, suffocating him. He struggled to breathe, but to no avail. He couldn't even use his arms like Brie to grab at his neck. An invisible force held them firmly in place.

Was this Val's power? Telekinesis? He'd heard of a few hunters who possessed such an ability, but he never expected it to be this dangerous.

The shortness of breath quickly got to Steve, and the lightheadedness set in. His vision rapidly shifted from clear to blurry, all while Val stood there, staring at him with folded hands. "You two are going to tell me everything. From start to finish."

Chapter 14

THE PLATINUM BROTHERS

"Brie!" Steve gasped, shooting up from the ground in a cold sweat. He took in quick, shallow breaths, unable to get enough oxygen.

"Mr. Gale?" He heard a familiar voice call out through the pounding of his heart. His vision was incredibly blurry, but he could still see that it was Brie.

Somehow, seeing her immediately calmed him down. As a result, his breathing slowed, and the hard pounding of his chest gradually lessened. "Oh, thank goodness, you're alright..." Steve groaned, rubbing his sore neck.

"What about you? Are you okay?" Brie asked, her face a look of concern.

"I-I'm fine. I think... What even happened?"

"You don't remember?"

Steve stared at Brie blankly before looking down at the metallic floor. All he remembered was Brie being in danger.

He closed his eyes, thinking hard. In seconds, the memories flooded back into him like a tsunami. "Now I do." He cleared his throat, looking back at his surroundings. "Where are we?"

Brie looked away. "I've been trying to figure that out for a while now. Still don't really know. I think we're on a ship?"

Finally, Steve's blurred vision fully cleared, allowing him to see what Brie was talking about. They were in a large room lined with glass walls, with the only visible entrance being a triangular door ahead of them. Aside from the flights of stairs leading up to a throne in the back, the room appeared to be barren. On the bright side, the lack of decoration was heavily outweighed by the gorgeous view of outer space.

Even though the blank void of space was littered with stars, Steve couldn't help but feel like there were significantly fewer stars present than what he was used to seeing in the night sky. Not to mention the lack of stellar bodies in view—The only thing Steve could see was a large blue sun, a tiny purple moon, and a moderately sized purple planet.

"Yeah. Definitely seems like we're on a ship." He agreed. In any other circumstances, he would've totally been psyched that this was happening. Sci-fi flicks were his jam as a child!

Steve finally took notice of what they were in. "Is this a cage?" He asked, partially expecting an answer but really just speaking to fill in the silence.

He and Brie appeared to be on a square metal platform that hovered a few feet off the floor. Hanging directly above them was another square platform, though nothing was holding it up. From the way both platforms were positioned, there should've been metal bars or at least glass encasing them, but there was nothing of the sort.

"I guess so," Brie answered. "I tried leaving, but something stops me every time. I can't even put a dent in the thing." She rubbed her knuckles, which looked awfully bruised.

If she couldn't break either platform, there was no chance Steve would be able to. Instead, he attempted to put his arm outside of either platform's reach. Like Brie described, the moment his hand passed the cage's boundaries, he found himself unable to push forward. An invisible force stopped him from extending any further. It felt akin to magnets repulsing one another.

Eventually, he gave up and leaned back. Whatever type of containment they were in, it was pretty effective. "Guess that explains why we weren't tied up," Steve commented, crossing his legs over one another to take up less space.

The two sat facing away from each other, with the only noise being the soft hum of the lights above. Although it was probably better for the both of them to keep quiet, Steve couldn't help but stir up a conversation.

"Noticed you were still in your uniform. Did you come straight to my house after work?"

Brie leaned backward, resting her back against Steve's.

"N-Nah. I was just taking a stroll through the city to clear my head. Then I ran into Ogenos and he told me what happened with you, and well, here I am."

"Sorry."

"What are you apologizing for?"

"For worrying you and the others. I should've called to let you guys know I was fine. I wasn't thinking straight."

"It's fine. Honestly, I'm just glad I made it in time to intercept that creepy dude. Even if I didn't end up saving you in the end..." she said in an embarrassed tone, chuckling awkwardly. "We were wondering why you wouldn't pick up any of our calls, but I'm guessing you had your hands tied with those bulls."

"Y-Yeah, you could say that." Steve's mood plummeted when he remembered what had happened at the warehouse. Brie somehow noticed his change in mood.

"What did those guys do to you?"

"What? Oh, nothing really. They just tied me to a chair."

"Really? 'Cause I doubt being tied to a chair causes you not to think straight."

Steve paused, thinking about how best to answer Brie. Seeing as they were stuck together, he figured it wouldn't hurt to be honest. "Ogenos killed them."

Steve felt Brie's body tense before quickly shifting. He didn't turn, but he guessed she was staring right at him.

"What?"

"He killed those minotaurs. Every last one of them. Samuel too. They didn't even stand a chance."

Brie slowly returned to leaning her back against Steve's, but there was a long pause before she responded with a baffled, "Damn..."

"I mean, after he killed that B-Tier tyrant, I knew he was strong. But I didn't think he was *that* strong. Or that mercil ess..."

"Wait, are you talking about the tyrant that appeared in Valentine Mall?"

"Yep."

"That was him?!"

"Yep." Steve really wished he could see the look on Brie's face, but right now, he didn't want to move any part of his body. Just thinking about everything that led to this moment exhausted him.

"If Ogenos did all of that, what does that Val Biox guy want with him?"

"Well, to catch you up to speed, Ogenos is not from Tyran. He's an alien."

"I knew there was something off about him!"

"He's not just any alien, though. Apparently, he's like some leader."

"Really?"

"I guess so. I only learned that part a few hours ago." Steve sighed, cursing himself for believing Ogenos's lies without even a hint of skepticism. That's what he gets for being so trusting and optimistic.

After another short pause, Brie responded. "So, what does Val want with us?"

Before Steve could take a guess, the triangular door suddenly glowed bright purple. It would then dissolve in a mystical display.

On the other side was none other than the Supreme General, Val Biox. "Ah, you're both awake. Excellent." He stepped inside. "I do hope you inferior lifeforms plan to cooperate this time. The alternative would be extremely painful... for you."

Brie quickly shifted onto her knees, looking about ready to cuss Val out. "What's your problem, dude? First, you break into Mr. Gale's house. Then, you kidnap both of us. Now, you—"

Val raised a finger, only for Brie's mouth to clamp shut mid-sentence. Anything she said afterward was muffled. "Enough of that." Despite his commands, Brie pried at her mouth in defiance. Unfortunately, it was for naught.

Steve had his suspicions after what happened at the house, but now he was certain Val had telekinetic abilities. "L-Look, I don't know what you want with us, but we mean no harm."

"As if you could harm superior beings such as us." Val taunted, stepping up to Steve and Brie's cage with all four arms folded behind his back.

The way he was posed reminded Steve of Ogenos, which prompted a sudden question: "What are you?"

Val's mandibles clicked slowly, as if he was wondering why Steve would ask such a thing. "Yes, I suppose our great civilization wouldn't exist in your pointless reality." He said, evidently talking to himself. No doubt, he and Ogenos were of the same species.

"Hear me, human, and..." Val's gaze shifted to Brie, who still struggled to get her mouth open. "Whatever you may be." He finished in a dismissive tone. "I am part of the mighty malfadian species. We are a race ruled by the one true supreme being, Sir Overlord. Though, you may know him as Ogenos Verum."

So it's true. Ogenos hadn't lied when he said he ruled an empire. But that begs the question, why would he leave?

"For committing the heinous crime of abducting our ruler, you two *will* suffer. However, should you come clean on what you did with him, I will ensure your ends are swift and painless."

"Hang on a second! What makes you think *we* kidnapped Og—" Val's eyes narrowed. "Er... your Sir Overlord?"

The general stared at him before clicking out a response. "What is your name, human?"

"S-Steve Gale."

"Ah, so that is why the Red One refers to you as Mr. Gale. Well, as I recall her saying, I broke into your place of residency. Is that true?"

"Well, it was more I opened the door for you like a dummy, but yeah."

"So, that primitive structure was indeed your living quarters. Sir Overlord's energy signature was riddled all over it. Does that not make you guilty?"

"Whoa, whoa. Look, I never said he didn't stay at my place. All I said was I didn't kidnap him! When I found him, he was already unconscious. I simply... dragged him back to my place..." Steve slowly realized he wasn't making the situation any better, even though he was telling the truth.

"Hm." Val raised one of his hands, about to snap his fingers.

"Wait!" Steve frantically waved his hands. "I know it sounds shady, but I'm being honest! I mean, think about it. Do I really seem capable of abducting your mighty leader?"

Val looked Steve up and down, probably gauging his strength. After a brief pause, he lowered his hand. "No. You seem quite harmless, in fact."

Steve let out an internal sigh of relief.

"But the Red One..." Val eyed Brie, who was blissfully un-aware of his gaze, as well as the entire conversation, due to her preoccupation with her mouth.

"Brie has nothing to do with this! She didn't even know your Sir Overlord was an alien. She was just in the wrong place at the wrong time."

Val's mandibles made another questioning clicking noise. Steve could only hope this meant Val was taking what he said into consideration, and hopefully realize this was all one big misunderstanding.

"Even if what you say is true, this does not explain his sudden disappearance." He stepped closer to the cage.

Steve wasn't sure what Val wanted him to say. It's not like he knew what Ogenos was thinking when he...

Wait... did Ogenos leave without saying a word to anyone? The answer seemed pretty obvious, but why? Why abandon the people you know and leave behind an empire you ruled?

Steve's pondering was interrupted when Brie finally got her mouth open, shouting at the top of her lungs. "I'm gonna kick your ass when we get out of here!" Brie lunged for Val, reaching out to choke the mess out of him. Unfortunately for her, the magnetic barrier holding them prisoner prevented her from getting close to the general.

He didn't even flinch and continued standing right out-side of her reach. Instead of getting angry, like Steve expect-

ed, he brought a hand up to his chin, stroking it quizzical-
ly. "Impressive." He murmured. "It seems I underestimated
you, Red One."

Wait, Val was impressed? That's an... odd reaction, to say
the least.

"Well, if you two won't talk willingly, then we'll just have
to—"

Sudden, booming sounds of alarms went off, cutting Val
off. The noise wasn't anything like what Steve was used to,
but he should've expected that from an alien ship.

"What now?" Val clicked in annoyance, using the datapad
on his wrist. After a few seconds of tapping, his irritated face
morphed into one of shock. "Intruders?"

Brie and Steve looked at each other, silently asking each
other for confirmation that they heard what they heard.

They all got their answer when a terrible scraping noise
screeched from the other side of the triangular door. Then,
rather than dissolving, the door instantly separated into
thousands of tiny mint-sized pieces, akin to being sliced
millions of times.

Two silhouettes cloaked in darkness stood on the other
side of the now-destroyed door. Something about their appearance looked oddly familiar to Steve.

"Director, I believe we've discovered the source of the
rifts," said one of the silhouettes. They stepped forward,

only to be stopped by the other silhouette, who'd then point at Val. "We've encountered another one of those tyrants. This one seems... different." Finally, the two newcomers stepped into the light.

"No way!" Steve gasped, recognizing them instantly. "Y-You're Silver Platinum!" He blurted, pointing to the figure that spoke. "And you're Platinum Platinum!" He announced, pointing to the other.

"Those are dumb names." Val clicked quietly, though Steve was too psyched to care about the general's rude comment.

Brie turned to Steve, looking rather perturbed. "W-Wait, aren't those guys apex hunters?"

"The top tenth and ninth!" Steve specified. "I can't believe this. *The* Platinum Brothers are actually here!"

It had been a dream of Steve's to meet an apex hunter in person, though he never thought it'd actually come true, let alone with the Platinum Brothers. Both hunters belonged to a prestigious family of elves, so they often kept to themselves.

Silver, the youngest brother, looked at Steve once he started freaking out with excitement. He was shorter and leaner than Platinum, possessing a more feminine face. Had it not been for their matching white hair and silver eyes, no one would think they were related.

"Brother, it appears these tyrants are holding two civilians captive."

Val crackled out a response. "I am a malfade."

Silver hesitated. "It talks."

"Not it, he." Val stepped away from the cage. "Now, explain yourselves for this intrusion."

"We've no desire to answer to tyrants." Silver's posture straightened out, and a more stoic expression overtook his face. "Since you can understand us, listen. You are to release those two civilians and hand over the device responsible for creating the rifts."

Val clicked in response yet again, only this time, his clicking sounded neither annoyed nor angry. He sounded... amused? "I get it now. You creatures are so lacking in evolution that you can't sense when you've met a higher power. A terrible shame."

Platinum brought out a rectangular device, waving it in Val's direction. It went off with a loud beep.

Silver opened his mouth, but Val continued before he could speak. "Ah, I see. You're looking for this?" A small compartment in his armor opened; out hovered a small blue orb covered in green symbols.

"Hand it over." Silver demanded.

Val laughed. "And what will you do if I don't?"

Silver smirked. "Guess nobody told you, tyrant. We're the

best of the best. And we're pretty good at killing your kind."

Val couldn't help but laugh more, which made Silver's smirk falter. "Is that right? You're the best warriors that insignificant civilization has to offer? Fine then. I suppose I can spare a few of my precious minutes to entertain you. I need to gauge the defenses of your planet anyway."

Silver huffed, putting two fingers to his ear. "Director, we've located the source of the rifts, but it's being protected by a tyrant. It's also holding two civilians captive. ...Negative. We're not sure of its tier. Maybe high-B to low-A? ...Understood." Silver unsheathed his blade, and Platinum followed suit.

"Finally done uttering nonsense? Very well." Val posed, outstretching all four of his arms with the blue orb hovering slightly above him. "Watch and weep, human and Red One. Your strongest heroes are about to fall to the immeasurable might of the Supreme General, Val Biox."

Chapter 15

THE TYRANTS

"Oh," Ogenos said blankly after bumping into a wooden sign. He'd been so lost in thought, he didn't realize where he was until now: Wing Park. "Back where I started, hm?"

He stared ahead at the dark and empty park, specifically the swing set. Something about the design intrigued him, so he went and sat on one. Despite its frail appearance, it supported his weight.

Once again, Ogenos found himself alone with his thoughts. The peaceful, quiet breeze of the cool wind eased him greatly, marred only by the distant sounds of the urban city.

Ogenos folded his hands together, still pondering why Steve got so upset over his actions. Sure, maybe he should've handled the situation delicately, but as far as he knew, any mortal would've appreciated being saved. The mother was when he saved her child, and so was Katie when he prevented her death. *So why wasn't Steve?*

Could the butchering of the Ragin' Bulls really have been

that bad? If they were bad people, why would it even matter? Besides, it seemed like the most logical thing to do at the time. He had the power, so why not use it? It was all so confusing...

"Ugh! Come on!" A shrill voice cut through the wind, making Ogenos jolt. Walking near the park's entrance was none other than Maya, dressed in extravagant clothing and all dolled up.

She angrily tapped away on her rectangular device, which he learned was a phone, before putting it to her ear. "Pick up the phone, Sam." She said in a demanding tone, huffing and puffing impatiently.

It was clear something had Maya in a sour mood, but quite frankly, Ogenos didn't care.

He closed his eyes, pretending she wasn't there. At least, he tried to pretend. It was pretty hard to ignore Maya when she constantly made noise, whether it be through the tapping of her feet or the repeated groans and sighs of irritation.

"Dammit," she muttered through gritted teeth. This Sam person obviously didn't answer her call.

Ogenos kept his eyes closed, expecting to hear Maya walk away. Instead, there was a long moment of silence.

Maya clicked her tongue, abruptly breaking the silence. "Hey, I know you."

Dammit. Ogenos opened his eyes; As he feared, she was

looking right at him.

Maya approached with a sway in her hips. "You're Stevie's friend," she stated, much to Ogenos's confusion.

"If you know this, why bother repeating the information?" Ogenos was hoping his bluntness would deter her from engaging in further dialogue.

To his dismay, Maya shrugged it off with a dry chuckle. She'd stuff her phone inside a small brown bag strapped to her shoulder before sitting on the swing next to him. "So, why're you here?"

It seemed ignoring her presence was no longer an option. "I wasn't aware I needed a reason to go places."

"Fair enough." Maya began slightly swinging back and forth with pursed red lips. "Samuel won't answer any of my calls, the jerk."

I never asked... Ogenos side-eyed her, starting to understand why Steve disliked the elf so much.

"...Wait, Samuel?" He turned to her after processing what she said. No way she was talking about him the whole time... right?

"Uh-huh. Can you believe it? The big bastard plans a date for tonight, then has the nerve to stand me up *and* dodge my calls! The audacity!" Maya stopped swinging, holding her hand up to the bright moon. "Do you know how long it took me just to get ready? Seriously, he may be a handsome hunk, but he has no idea how lucky he is."

Maya's complaints entered one non-existent ear and exited the other, as Ogenos couldn't help but think about Samuel's rotting carcass in that abandoned warehouse.

Why was he suddenly so nervous? Was it because Maya had close ties with the bull and would, no doubt, be mad should she discover the truth? It wasn't like Ogenos was afraid of what she would do to him... Or maybe he was? No, he definitely was.

His nervousness stemmed from the possibility she might report him if she discovered what happened to Samuel. Sure, he could kill her to prevent that from ever happening, but if he kept up with these reckless actions, he'd eventually be back to square one.

Besides, he'd like to refrain from hurting Maya. Even though they weren't together anymore, Ogenos suspected Steve would be furious at him if her blood was on his hands.

"Are you listening?"

Ogenos snapped out of his thoughts, seeing Maya now staring at him. "Sorry, I didn't know you wanted me to listen to your babble."

Maya pouted, only for her gaze to trail downward. "What happened there?"

Though there was minimal light in the park, the shining moon provided just enough visibility to expose how tattered

Ogenos's shirt was, once again making it the highlight of the conversation.

"Samuel." He blurted in a flustered tone.

"Samuel?" Maya repeated, her ears wiggling attentively.

IDIOT! Ogenos shouted at himself, wanting to bash his stupid face into the metal swing set.

Thanks to his flustered behavior, he drove the conversation onto the very topic he wanted to avoid. What was going on with him? He hadn't been this nervous in centuries!

...No use crying about it now.

It'd be too suspicious if he left it off there. He'll just have to do what he does best: lie.

"I... ran into Samuel a while ago. We got into a big fight."

"Oh... I guess that makes sense. Samuel really hates you, y'know." After a short pause, Maya squinted her eyes in suspicion.

Ogenos waved his upper hands defensively, not giving her the chance to make assumptions. "Don't look at me like that! I merely defended myself from his hostile actions. That is all!" He swore, rubbing his lower hands together. "The truth is, I won. He got pretty embarrassed about it. The next thing I knew, he packed up and left the city."

"Left the city?!" Maya gasped. "Without me!?"

"Yes. I even caught him as he was leaving and questioned him about his decision regarding you. All he said was he couldn't care less."

Ogenos's false story seemed to spark something within Maya. Her face turned a shade of red, nearly matching Brie's complexion. "That fucking..." she seethed, whipping out her phone in an instant.

Ogenos crackled a small sigh of relief. The anxious sensation deep in his stomach kept him from coming up with a good story, and he more or less blurted out the first thoughts that came to mind. Luckily, Maya was gullible enough to believe his half-baked lies.

Now that Ogenos was in the clear, he focused back on Maya, watching her type on her phone much more aggressively than she had previously. "What are you doing?"

"Sam wants to abandon his girl because of his shattered manhood? Fine by me! He doesn't know what he'll be missing out on." She answered without skipping a beat. "And done. Break-up text sent. Good riddance!" Maya finished, tossing her phone back in her bag.

Ogenos didn't think she'd be so hasty in such a decision, especially considering Samuel was a gang leader. Then again, he wouldn't complain about it either.

"Well, now that it's just the two of us, how about you and I get to know each other a bit more and...link up?" Maya said in an odd tone, leaning in closer to Ogenos.

"Link up?" He turned to her, puzzled.

"Yeah! You're big, assertive, and incredibly strong! Not just anyone can beat Sam, you know. A guy like you is perfect for a girl like me." She praised and cooed.

It was only then that Ogenos understood what she was suggesting; the idea unsettled him. It wasn't as though the proposal nauseated him. The problem was he hardly knew anything about Maya, not to mention she seemed to move on from Samuel *way* too quickly. Plus, he could see Steve being opposed to the idea anyway.

"I'll pass." Ogenos turned away, earning a slight giggle from Maya. It wasn't a laugh of awkwardness or anything like that, but rather confidence.

Before he knew it, she hopped out of her swing and stood a few feet in front of him with crossed arms. A big, arrogant smile spread across her face—one which made him sick. "I know you're new and all to the city. I also know you're a smart guy. Smart enough to know when a once-in-a-life-time opportunity is standing right in front of him."

Maya shook her head, swinging her luscious blonde hair over her shoulder. "You see, my family is rich. Like, stupid rich. I can give you any and everything you want."

The proposal immediately lost any value it might've had once those words left Maya's mouth. "Any and everything?" He repeated with a small click of his mandibles.

She smirked, believing to have piqued his interest. "Any

and everything."

Ogenos stood from his swing, staring down at Maya. "In that case, how about leaving me alone?"

He watched as Maya's confident facade crumbled into a bewildered expression. Satisfied, he walked past her, intending to leave the park.

Maya let him get three steps away before scrambling ahead of him, blocking his path. Ogenos only stopped after catching a whiff of some intoxicating, odd-smelling perfume. The smell, which he assumed was meant to be pleasant, assaulted his nostrils like a gas attack. How he went so long without smelling the perfume was beyond him—he could barely hold back his coughs.

"H-Hey, idiot! Can't you see when pure gold is standing right in front of you?" Ogenos looked her up and down, not seeing what was pure or gold about her. "Seriously? What's wrong with you? You're lucky I'm even offering! There's plenty of guys who'd kill to have even a minute with a bombshell like me."

"Then why don't you seek those 'guys' out? After all, I'm certain I have nothing to offer you."

Maya snickered, waving a finger in front of Ogenos. "That's not true." She hummed softly, regaining her smile. "Sam's gonna be *so* mad when I post us together on all my socials. Serves him right, too. He should've never left me behind." Maya paused. "Well, I guess I should've expected him to do something this stupid in hindsight. Minotaurs aren't really the brightest."

"What makes you think Samuel will even care? He was *willing* to leave you, after all."

Maya responded with a mischievous giggle that sounded borderline sinister. "If there's one thing I know about guys, they *always* care. Besides, I'm sure Steve will be thrilled to know the girl he neglected is being taken care of by one of his big, strong friends."

Maya practically swooned over the thought of damaging her exes emotionally. Ogenos wasn't sure if he should be concerned with her disturbing mindset, disgusted by her clear intent, impressed by her vile tactics, or all three.

Steve was right. Maya was wicked... She was also very foolish.

Blatantly explaining how she would use Ogenos for her own satisfaction and thinking he'd be okay with it? Absurd. If there was one thing he disliked more than being unhappy, it was being used by another. Besides, he could see how her story would pan out. How could he not? It seemed all too familiar, like looking at a mirror.

"Why don't you find some other bootlicker to use."

"Use? No, no. You misunderstand my proposal! This would be a mutually beneficial arrangement."

"Mutually beneficial, how?"

"You're really asking me that? Well, let's see, in exchange for you just being you, you get loads of money, a hot elf, and, again, any and everything you want. What more could you want?"

"I see what you're doing. So, to save you the trouble, I'll let you know now that it won't work."

Maya raised a brow. "What won't work?"

"The fleeting feeling you get from tormenting others. It won't satisfy you. Not in the long run."

The confusion on Maya's face hadn't disappeared, but it gained a hint of concern. "What are you..."

"You know what I'm talking about." His mandibles clicked aggressively as he leaned in closer to Maya.

"I had wondered why you enjoyed interacting with Steve back at the mall, even though it seemed as though your relationship ended in disaster. But now I see. You don't enjoy interacting with the toys you break. You enjoy tormenting them."

Maya grimaced, which didn't stop Ogenos from continuing. "You have an abundance of wealth. There isn't a thing you want that you can't get. But perhaps that is why you feel empty and unfulfilled. You think tormenting those you once held close will bring you joy? Well, maybe it will. But that gratification is always short-lived. Ultimately, you will always feel discontent."

Maya crossed her arms and looked away. "Q-Quit spouting nonsense. What do you know about me anyway? You're just an insectoid from those closed-knit colonies." She clicked her tongue, pure annoyance seeping through her tone.

Even though she tried desperately to hide it, Ogenos saw right through her. He was dead-on about everything he said—a fact he already knew. "Lie to yourself all you want, elf. But I see. You're so unsatisfied with your life that you only find joy when others are unable to enjoy their own."

He stood up straight, crossing all four arms. "Maybe, just maybe, if you thought about changing your approach, I could've been the next Steve or Samuel—Just another toy to break and torment for your own satisfaction. But no. You could never think about doing anything different, could you? The only thing you can think about is..." Ogenos stopped, noticing a faint tear stream down Maya's cheek. "...Yourself."

Maya turned away, showing Ogenos her backside. "Y'know what? I don't need a dense knucklehead as a boyfriend anyway." She said, her voice brimming with anger. He could sense that wasn't how she truly felt. She wouldn't be sniffling otherwise. "Later." Maya rushed out of the park, losing the graceful sway in her steps.

Ogenos stood as stiff as a statue, completely stunned—but not because of the outcome his words brought.

Although he struck a nerve in Maya's core, in doing so, the final piece to his puzzle had been found; a revelation dawned on him.

Despite the little time he spent with her, Ogenos couldn't deny that Maya's wealth, status, and especially her pompous attitude, were all too familiar. She might as well have been his less-powerful interdimensional counterpart.

Funnily enough, Maya had the most traits he disliked out of everyone else he'd met thus far. Even more than Samuel. That said, it was only through evaluating her personality that he finally pieced together what his problem was: his selfishness.

Once Ogenos had a thirst for power, he couldn't stop drinking. Everything he'd ever done was to fuel his own ambitions, whether it'd be for him directly or for his empire. Though, no matter what he did, his thirst never quenched. Even when he sought to undo what he *thought* was the source of his dissatisfaction, all he ever really did was continue his same habits in a different universe.

He lacked selflessness... No. He lacked empathy, something his body had tried to tell him for centuries. What else would explain his overreaction to Steve's abduction? Or his sudden urge to save Katie? Or that gratifying sensation from when the mother thanked him?

Even now, he felt it with Maya. He knew what she was going through, and yet he used his words as a cleaver, hacking away at her heart without care. He should've been more considerate of her feelings.

Even though Maya deserved and needed the harsh dose of reality, apologizing to her in the near future would be the right thing to do. For now, however, there was somebody else he owed an apology.

It was a short trip from Wing Park to Steve's house. Thankfully, the two locations were in the same neighborhood—not that distance would've been an issue. He just wanted to use the transit time to think about how he'd apologize.

That all changed the moment he laid eyes on Steve's house. He couldn't explain how or why, but he immediately knew something was off.

Steve's car was still missing, and one of the front windows was covered by a cardboard box, but none of that was what set him off.

Upon getting closer, Ogenos noticed the front door

cracked open—a quiet invitation for anyone to enter. "Was he expecting me?" His mandibles clicked slowly, thinking how that conflicted with what Steve told him earlier.

With little else to go off of, he entered.

The wall in front of the door had a big dent in its center, with many cracks spreading from the impact. Something about the sight was wrong.

"Steve?" Ogenos called out, feeling a terrible anxiousness course through him. As he feared, no response.

He took a few steps in, only to pause upon sensing the energy signature of two others. The first of which was Brie, which he couldn't say was out of the ordinary, considering the relationship with Steve and his coworkers. However, what threw him for a loop was the energy signature of Val.

It had to be a mistake... Perhaps he simply missed his Supreme General so much that he started mistaking someone else's aura for his. It certainly made more sense.

"Steve?" Ogenos called out again, hoping for something—anything. However, as he walked further inside, the only thing he heard was the sound of the TV coming from the living room. He stepped inside to find it completely vacant.

The confusion he felt bubbled to the surface, replacing his anxiety. Whatever happened at the front entrance never made it further into the house, evidently. So, what happened in the first place?

"In other news, reports are coming in that the rifts appearing around Valentina City have become less frequent after the past hour." Ogenos turned to the TV, giving it his full attention. "The Hunter Agency has yet to make an official statement, but it can be assumed that the top tenth and ninth apex hunters, A.K.A, the Platinum Brothers, are making progress!"

The news reporter sounded enthusiastic. Not only that, but it appeared to be one of the same reporters from before. Do they ever sleep?

Never mind them. Something else stuck out to Ogenos: The rifts. This wasn't the first time he'd heard of them, and the more he thought about it, the more things pieced together.

If he really had been sensing Val's energy here of all places, then it could only mean one thing. "Steve's in trouble."

Chapter 16

SIR OVERLORD

Slash, thrust, swipe, and dash—the most frequent actions performed by the Platinum Brothers. It was a miracle Steve could keep up with them. They were so fast, they almost appeared as blurs.

He hadn't expected Silver to move as fast as he did, especially since he was covered neck to toe in smooth, thin silver armor, the weight of which should've slowed him.

In contrast, Platinum was not only without armor, but also without a shirt. All he wore were black leggings that had chains acting as the belt and large steel boots with spikes protruding from their underside. And yet, he was noticeably slower.

Admittedly, Steve was focused less on the fight and more on the Platinum Brothers themselves. It was his first time witnessing an apex-hunter in live action. He was going to get the most out of this experience if it was the last thing he did.

However, ever since the fight started, he noticed something was off.

Silver and Platinum were obviously going for killing blows, but Val didn't seem to be taking the fight seriously. Steve thought the brothers could use that to their advantage, with their quick speed and all, but neither could land a decisive blow on the alien general.

It didn't make sense to Steve. Val wasn't moving even half as fast as the hunters. In fact, his movements were slow and deliberate. Surprisingly, however, they were also unpredictable.

"Quick ones, aren't you?" Val clicked in slight amusement.

"How?" Silver grunted in frustration, thrusting his blade at Val's chest. Although the attack was blindingly fast, Val somehow dodged by slowly sidestepping.

"First time encountering a superior being?" Val asked tauntingly, causing Silver to furrow his brows and grit his teeth.

Silver pulled away, and Platinum dove in to deliver a jumping overhead strike. Steve wasn't sure when or how he jumped so high, but Val stayed put, not even looking up at the descending hunter.

When Platinum's blade was inches away from making contact with Val's skull, it stopped mid-air. Platinum's body jerked when his weapon's momentum suddenly vanished; he hung from the blade's handle, dangling in the air like some poor feline stuck on a tree branch.

"Oh, and you were so close." Val laughed, finally looking up at Platinum. "Looks like you'll have to try a—" Platinum kicked upward, striking him right in the mouth and making him stumble backward.

At the same time, the telekinetic force holding Platinum's blade broke, allowing the hunter to swing away from Val and land next to Silver elegantly.

"Woo!" Steve couldn't help but cheer.

"You talk too much." Said Platinum, his voice low and firm.

Val's mandibles clicked rapidly, creating an odd noise akin to teeth chattering. Steve expected him to be furious, but he looked mildly irritated rather than flat-out angry. "Lucky hit." He straightened his posture, and the chattering noise ceased.

Val flicked his wrist, and numerous small purple balls materialized on either side of him. They hummed lowly and subtly vibrated the surrounding air.

Without warning, the balls rained down on Silver and Platinum like a blizzard. Both brothers deflected the shots as fast as they came at them, scattering the projectiles everywhere.

"Steve!" Brie yelped before hugging Steve, using her larger stature to shield him from the incoming projectiles.

Luckily for both of them, the same magnetic force keeping them trapped also kept other entities out. Any purple ball that hit the invisible wall of their cage would simply bounce back, causing them and their containment no harm.

By the time Val's attack ended, scorch marks dotted the room everywhere. It was a miracle the glass walls hadn't shattered. In fact, unlike the ceiling and floor, they were the only things that came out of the ordeal unscathed—Aside from the Platinum Brothers, of course.

That was the first blow either brother had landed on Val since the battle started, and from the looks of it, all it did was annoy him. Still, like every other attack he'd thrown, Silver and Platinum came out unharmed.

Steve couldn't even get mad at the stalemate. He was having far too much fun from just spectating the fight.

However, he also couldn't deny that ominous feeling floating in the back of his head. The Platinum Brothers were trying their best to dispose of Val like they would any tyrant, but he was simply toying with them. He could end this fight whenever he wanted, and they didn't seem to realize that...

"I grow tired of this stalemate," Val announced, folding his arms behind his back. "I must say, I'm impressed you were able to make it this far into the ship undetected. Especially with the rather underwhelming display you've shown thus far. But I wonder, is this truly the best you can offer? If so,

I'm afraid our playtime ends here."

Silver and Platinum hardened their stances, ready to launch into another assault. Before they could, a new voice entered the fray. "Stop." Everyone turned.

Steve was the first to stammer a response. "Ogenos?!"

Val was next. "Sir Overlord!" Ogenos stood in front of the destroyed triangular door, wearing nothing but the same tattered clothes from the warehouse. "What are you wearing...?"

"Never mind that." Ogenos waved his hand before surveying the scene before him. He stared at everyone for a long moment before his eyes furrowed. "What is happening here?"

"Sir Overlord, we've been searching for you! I managed to track down and capture the culprits behind your abduction, but these two newcomers interrupted my interrogation."

"Abduction? Nobody abducted me."

Val tilted his head; his mandibles clicked slowly. "But... your presence was littered all over the human's residence?" He said uncertainly, pointing to Steve.

Silver butted in, interrupting whatever Ogenos was about to say. "Plat, this tyrant feels different." He said, clearly addressing Ogenos, which Val *did not* like.

"You will address Sir Overlord with dignity and respect, you miserable—"

Ogenos raised a hand, instantly quelling Val's outburst. "And who might you be?"

"Ogenos!" Steve blurted. "Those are apex hunters! Do not hurt them!"

Silver side-eyed Steve. "Hurt us?" he started, sounding insulted. "I'd be worried about what we'll do to it. And anyway, why are you speaking to this tyrant so casually?" Now Silver was looking at Steve with skepticism in his eyes.

Steve didn't want to have one of his idols view him with suspicion, but at the same time, he couldn't stop himself from defending Ogenos. "He's not a tyrant! He's just a person! Granted, a person who's made some mistakes... a lot of mistakes actually, but we all have at some point, right?!"

"No," Platinum spoke, his eyes never once leaving Ogenos. "D-Don't lie!"

"There is only one *person* who has this much power. And this tyrant is not her." Platinum clarified, which only confused Steve more, ironically enough.

Amidst his confusion, he noticed something off about Platinum. He was unusually serious compared to earlier, and there was a hint of concern in his eyes. Platinum hadn't acted this way before, even when they were fighting Val... It disturbed Steve greatly.

His concern was not unfounded, as even Silver commented on Platinum's mood change. "Plat, you're giving this thing *that* look. Don't tell me its power is..." The eldest simply nodded, still not turning away from Ogenos. He didn't even dare to blink. Silver exhaled a long, shaky breath. "So, what's the plan? Should we kill it or report back to headquarters?"

Fear shot through Steve like a bullet. He couldn't explain why he was so tense when it came to Ogenos—or was he fearing for the hunters? Either way, he opened his mouth to shout.

"It's fine, Steve," Said Ogenos, looking over at him. "I'll handle this." It was like he could sense Steve's uneasiness.

His assurance made it seem like he wouldn't take the hostile approach, so Steve trusted him—not that he had any other choice.

Now that the others remained quiet, the Platinum Brothers' gaze fell solely on Ogenos. He had the floor, though he was unsure what to do with it.

When he pieced together what was going on at Steve's house, he rushed to find the nearest portal, appearing in one of the lower sections of the malfadian mothership. When he traced Val's energy signature back to his throne room, he didn't expect to find more than Val and Steve.

He wouldn't bother asking how Brie got wrapped up in all of this. However, he was curious as to what the two elves were doing. Steve referred to them as apex hunters. They didn't look or feel quite as intimidating as he imagined. But if they were hunters, they must've been the same ones from the news.

"You must be the Platinum Brothers," Ogenos noted, causing Silver to perk up.

"You know us?"

"A little."

"Then you know what's about to happen to you." Silver's stance stiffened in tandem with his words.

Usually, Ogenos wouldn't waste any more time on fools like him, but he wasn't that kind of person anymore. He didn't want to be. "Hang on." He raised his four hands defensively, slowly walking to the side. Silver and Platinum traced his every move. "I do not wish to fight."

"All you tyrants are the same. Even the ones that can talk. If you're trying to make us lower our guard with feigned friendliness, drop the act and just attack."

"I'm not feigning anything!" Ogenos declared, now positioned behind the glass wall of his throne room. He pointed behind the Platinum Brothers at Steve. "Steve is correct. I am not a tyrant. I am not your enemy."

"I've heard enough," Platinum spoke, his tone decisive

and unwavering. It seemed like no matter what anyone said, these hunters would not listen to reason.

Before Ogenos could get another word in, Platinum rushed forward with a burst of speed. His sudden attack must've been an impulsive one, as even Silver was shocked at how quickly he moved. Surely, the elf was moving at incomprehensible speeds, considering Steve, Brie, and even Val hadn't reacted. However, for Ogenos, Platinum might as well have been moving in slow-motion.

He caught the blade with ease, surprising Platinum. "If I wanted to hurt you, I would've already done it,"

There was a sudden, brief period of silence. During which, Ogenos examined the blade Platinum used. Something about its appearance intrigued him.

The blade was platinum in color, with sparkling blue diamonds adorning its center. Unlike the blade, the handle was golden and engraved with glimmering red rubies.

This is pleasing to the eyes. Ogenos clicked quietly, having most of his attention fall onto the beautiful blade. Although the blade was far too small for him to use as a weapon, he desperately wished Platinum didn't possess ownership of it.

"Platinum!" Silver shouted, snapping Ogenos back into the moment.

Apparently, Platinum had been tugging at his blade, which was firmly in Ogenos's hand, for far too long. He hadn't realized his grip was that tight.

Before Ogenos could let go, Platinum released his sword and kicked off of him. Despite the force of the kick, it didn't move him, nor was it felt. However, as Platinum jumped out of the way, Ogenos caught a quick glimpse of another weapon coming at him.

It was another sword, yet curvier and a tad bit darker in color. It wasn't quite as pleasing to the eye, so Ogenos side-stepped out of its way, allowing it to whoosh right past him.

"Really, there's no need for violence," Ogenos said calmly, only to hear a faint cracking noise behind him.

Upon turning, he saw Silver's blade lodged into the glass wall, with cracks sprawling from the impact. A sight that wouldn't be too out of the ordinary, if it weren't for the fact that the glass walls on the mothership were made specifically to handle cosmic phenomenons, like the explosion of a dying star. Ogenos should know—he tested it himself.

These are much sharper than I thought. Ogenos looked down at Platinum's blade, wondering what else it could cut through.

Meanwhile, the cracking noise grew louder, and the cracks spread wider. Before they knew it, the glass wall shattered; with that, the vacuum of space violently sucked out everything from the room, air and all.

Although Ogenos was closest to the suction, he barely felt a thing. The same could not be said for the Platinum Brothers, who were sucked out like water down a drain. Their screams were silenced almost instantly.

Before anyone else was pulled out into space, metal walls slammed overtop the broken glass, stopping the immense suction immediately.

Only after everything was said and done did Ogenos realize he could've caught both hunters. "Stupid..." He facepalmed himself, looking down at the blade Platinum left behind. *At least I can keep it now.*

"Apologies, Steve. I tried to stop them." He turned, seeing Steve wasn't as mad as he expected. More so saddened.

"I know." He said in a knowing tone.

Val looked between the two for a second before bursting out in surprise. "Sir Overlord! What is the meaning of this?!"

Ogenos looked at Val. "What?"

"Apologizing to this furless mammal and holding back against your assailants! Especially after suffering such disrespect! This isn't like you at all..."

Ogenos grumbled, only because he was right.

In Val's defense, Ogenos had just up and left everything behind without so much as an explanation. Despite leaving his general to deal with the aftermath of his disappearance, Val went out of his way to look for Ogenos, even if that meant sifting through a possibly infinite multiverse...

He looked for him.

All this time, Ogenos had thought Val moved on. In reality, even after he abandoned him, Val never did the same.

That fact hurt more than a gamma ray ever could.

If anyone deserved an explanation, it was his Supreme General. "You're right, Val. This isn't like me at all. That's because... I'm not me."

Val clicked aggressively, turning to Steve and Brie. "Monsters! What did you do to our beloved leader?"

"Nothing," Ogenos answered for them. "They did nothing."

Val's four purple eyes curled in confusion and fear. "B-But Sir Overlord! These inferior lifeforms stole you from us, did they not?"

Ogenos shook his head. "They did no such thing. They aren't capable. I left on my own accord."

"On... your own accord...?" A look of abrupt realization flashed across Val's face, followed by a silent pause. "...W hy?"

Ogenos said nothing, instead burying the tip of the Platinum's sword into the floor. He walked to the other side of the throne room, stopping in front of the uncracked glass wall.

"I was tired," he finally answered, folding his arms behind

his back. "This monotonous routine of subjugation. Of des
truction..." Ogenos stared out at the twinkling sea of stars,
noting how sparse his universe's constellations were compared to Steve's universe. "I couldn't keep doing it. So, when
the transporter was presented to me, I saw my opportunity,
and I...left." Val's reflection saddened; Ogenos didn't dare
turn around to face him. He couldn't.

"I arrived on a planet called Tyran. The human you captured, Steve Gale, was my guide. Through him, I sought to
live life as an inferior lifeform, as I thought their lifestyle was
the solution to my problem." Ogenos lowered his head in
shame, clicking his mandibles in a melancholic rhythm. "It
is only recently that I realized the futility of my mission, for I
now understand what separates me from the likes of Steve.
Where he is selfless, I am selfish. Where he is strong, I am
weak. Where he is superior, I am... inferior."

Finally, Ogenos turned around, staring Val directly in the
eyes. "I do not regret leaving, Val. However, I do regret the
way I left." He crackled, clenching his fists. "If anyone, I
should've told you. Instead, I turned my back and abandoned the ones most loyal to me... That is my failure as a
leader."

"No, Sir Overlord!" Val cried out, prostrating himself before Ogenos. "It is my failure as Supreme General! Out of all
your servants, I am the closest to you, and yet, I still couldn't

see the emptiness gnawing at you from inside. I was a fool to be so shortsighted."

"That's—"

"Please, Sir Overlord, let me finish. I beg you." Val pleaded with an intensity that surprised Ogenos. Out of respect for his general's wishes, he remained silent.

"It was you who brought unification to our universe. So it will be you who will lead us into a new golden age." Val somehow lowered himself further onto the floor. "If conquering displeases you, then we will no longer conquer. If destroying planets displeases you, then we will no longer destroy." He looked up at Ogenos, revealing the tears flowing from his four eyes. "Your will is our command, and we will follow you, no matter what. So please, Sir Overlord... don't abandon us."

Ogenos stared at Val, furious. But he wasn't mad at his subordinate. He was mad at himself.

How could he be so foolish?

To think all his problems would be solved if he simply left...

To believe those closest to him would never understand or agree with how he felt...

And to think, once, he thought himself worthy of the title 'Sir Overlord.' Not anymore.

He was naïve, close-minded, and incompetent. Val was

none of those. "Rise, Val Biox." He commanded. "It is unfit for a Supreme General to kneel before an inferior."

"Don't say such blasphemous things, Sir Overlord!"

"It is not blasphemy if it is true." Ogenos turned his head, unable to look at Val without overwhelming shame. "You might never believe it, but I've lost the right to call myself Sir Overlord." He paused, realizing how weak he was, even now.

If he couldn't stand to look at his own general, how would he ever hope to remedy things?

...No.

He refused to just give up. Such an act didn't suit him. He might've lost the right to call himself Sir Overlord now, but he would earn it again. He had to.

Ogenos clicked with finality, turning his head back to look at Val. "Instead of trusting my legion, my first thought was to flee. A supreme being doesn't run from their problems. They overcome them." He began walking over to Val. "I will overcome any obstacle thrown my way, as I had before. Only this time, I will better myself and my legion." He stopped in front of his general, extending a hand to him. "I abandoned you once. Never again."

His promise caused even more tears to flow from Val, only this time, they were of happiness. He took Ogenos's hand graciously, clicking happily as he got off the floor.

From now on, Ogenos swore to do things differently. But before any of that...

"Steve." Ogenos turned, approaching Steve and Brie's magnetic cage. "I owe you an apology as well. Not just for what happened at the warehouse, but for everything. You showed me kindness and hospitality, and in return, I exploited your compassion, all for my own gain." He shook his head shamefully, ridden with guilt. "I should've handled Samuel and his crew delicately. But more importantly, I shouldn't have lied to you..."

Steve frowned.

"I understand if you no longer wish to keep me in your company. I...will return you and Brie back home and refrain from entering your universe ever again...if that is what you wish."

"Ogenos..." Steve quavered. "When I met you, I didn't think you were some genocidal maniac. Well, truth is, I didn't know. Still, you made some pretty bad decisions and... said some pretty horrible stuff." Ogenos's mood lowered, seeing where this was going. "But y'know what? You've proven that you want to change."

"I... Have?" Ogenos perked up, not expecting that response at all.

"Yeah. I mean, aside from that whole exchange between you and Val, you didn't try to kill the Platinum Brothers like you did Samuel. I don't know how you found us or knew what was going on, but you came looking for us—just like you came looking for me when Samuel's gang snatched me up. I don't know about you, but no selfish person does that. I was just... too caught up in my feelings to see that."

Steve scooted closer to Ogenos. "Look, I'm not gonna sit up here and pretend that you having a change of heart excuses everything you did. I mean, destroying planets? Enslaving people? I don't even wanna think of that stuff... But, if you really, and I mean *really*, want to forsake that way of life... then I'd be more than happy to help you."

Steve looked to the side. "Besides, you are the only person to have done something about Samuel. Yeah, it could've been handled better, but who knows? With me helping you, you'll probably do a whole lot more for Valentina City. Maybe even Tyran as a whole."

"You... You mean that?"

"He wouldn't say it if he didn't." Brie chimed. "Steve is a good man. That's what makes him special." Ogenos and Steve remained silent, staring at Brie. "...D-Don't make it awkward."

Steve laughed. "She's right, though. I wouldn't say something like that if I wasn't serious about it. I think everyone deserves a second chance, after all."

"But what about those hunters? Won't issues arise if I

remain with you?"

"Eh, maybe. I don't know how the HA is gonna respond to the death of two apex-class hunters. But it's not like you killed them or anything. I think we'll be fine. ...Probably..."

Overwhelming amounts of joy flooded through Ogenos. The prospect of Steve remaining by his side made him so happy, it left him speechless. "I don't know what to say..."

"Well, how about we start with you getting me and Brie out of here?" Steve chuckled, knocking on the bottom floor of the magnetic cage.

His mandibles clicked slowly, showing his mild embarrassment. "Right."

Chapter 17

FRESH START

"Good news, Valentina! Our portal troubles are no more, thanks to the valiant efforts of the Platinum Brothers!" The news reporter announced with joy.

It had been a few days since the whole debacle inside the malfadian mothership. As per Ogenos's instructions, the gateways connecting his universe to Tyran have been closed. Like Steve said, that seemed to be enough to put the locals at ease. However...

"Speaking of, they have yet to come out and make an official statement detailing their experience on the other side. However, The Hunter Agency has assured those concerned that our hunters are getting the proper rest they deserve!" The reporter cleared their throat. "In other news, word has gotten out that remaining members of the Ragin' Bulls have—"

Ogenos's mandibles crackled as he turned to Steve, who was in nothing but pajamas. "Why has your Hunter Agency not come out with the truth about those elves?"

"It's not like they know what happened. Otherwise, I'm pretty sure we would've gotten a visit." He slouched back on the couch. "Besides, I'm not sure they want to report to the public that two of their best hunters suddenly vanished."

"Would it be bad if they did?"

"Bad is an understatement. Last I checked, they haven't lost an apex hunter from anything other than retirement in the last three hundred years. Isn't that right, Brie?"

Ogenos looked to his other side, where Brie mindlessly scrolled through her phone.

She'd been frequenting Steve's house every day and staying for long periods ever since that incident. Ogenos once assumed the reason was because she worried for Steve's well-being. Now, however, he was certain Brie's visits were because of something else. Or rather, *someone* else.

"Huh? O-Oh, yeah. I think?" She looked up, obviously oblivious to the conversation.

Steve leaned back. "Point is, if the Hunter Agency announced that two of their apex hunters died, everyone would freak."

Ogenos squinted his eyes at Steve. "For someone who watched them perish, you sure seem unbothered..."

He replied with an exhausted sigh. "To be honest, I'm surprised myself. This has probably been the most hectic week of my life, and I'm not reacting how I thought I would. I think I'm becoming desensitized to it all." Steve sounded uncertain, emphasizing the quizzical look on his face.

"That's—" A loud crash cut Ogenos off.

Everyone turned around to see Val, along with a bunch of dropped items. Judging by the scene, he had bumped into the dresser, knocking everything off it. "Oh, apologies." He clicked sincerely, using his telekinesis to put the items back in their original spot.

Brie grunted softly. Ogenos subtly glanced at her, seeing her squinting at Val. *I knew it.* He clicked softly, suspecting Brie still had her suspicions about Val.

Funnily enough, Steve didn't seem all that bothered by Val's presence. Not like Brie was.

Ogenos sighed, getting off the couch and approaching Val. "Why are you still here?" At this point, he figured the general had overstayed his welcome.

"I told you, didn't I? As Supreme General, it is my responsibility to keep you safe."

"And as you can see, I am."

"For now, yes. But how long will that remain? I can't possibly keep you safe indefinitely if we're universes apart."

Ogenos grumbled, finding Val's protective nature to be a bit bothersome. He supposed it was warranted, considering the stunt he pulled. But if anyone, Val should've known Ogenos was the last person who needed protection.

"So what are you proposing? You staying here?" Ogenos said with a half-chuckle, partially joking. However, he got his answer when Val didn't respond. "Did you at least ask Steve? This is his residence, after all."

"Actually, he did," Steve answered. "Came up to me yesterday about it. I have the space for him, so it should be fine."

"Wha—Hold on a minute!" Brie interjected. "You're letting him stay with you?"

"Y-Yeah?"

"Are you forgetting that he threatened to kill us a few days ago?!"

"I know, I know. But that was a misunderstanding! It's water under the bridge now."

Brie scoffed. "You gotta stop being so nice! One of these days, it'll backfire on you."

I think it already has. Ogenos got reminded of Maya for some reason.

"Sir Overlord, the babbling of these lifeforms is incredibly tiring. How do you manage?" Val whispered.

Ogenos stared at the two conversing on the couch. In the past, he would've wholeheartedly agreed with Val. Now, he couldn't help but find amusement in their back and forth. "You get used to it."

"If you're so worried about it, you could stay too." Steve offered.

Brie's breath hitched in her throat. "R-Really?"

"Well, yeah! I mean, I didn't get this big house for nothing. I don't have much stuff either, so I've got plenty of rooms." Steve stopped himself. "Uh, I mean, you don't have to. I just figured it made sense since you're the only other person to know about this whole alien stuff..."

"N-No! I'll move in!" She accepted before Steve could take the invite back. "It'd beat having to drive here every day..."

Ogenos clicked slowly, finding Brie's tone to be odd. Not to mention, she averted her gaze from Steve when she spoke. It was painfully obvious the reason she gave wasn't actually why she accepted his offer so fast.

For now, he'd put his suspicions of Brie on the back burner. The mention of driving reminded him of something more important. "Steve, did you ever find your red SUV?"

"What? Oh, no. Not yet."

Steve told Ogenos he had reported his car as stolen on the same day they returned from the mothership. He didn't tell the authorities who stole it. Why? He wouldn't tell Ogenos that either. Either way, so far, it seemed as though his car vanished after the Ragin' Bulls did who knows what with it.

Despite losing his sole method of transportation, Steve seemed unbothered. Ironically, that bothered Ogenos. "How will you get to and from work now?"

Steve raised a brow. "Happy Burgers is closed, remember?"

Ogenos lowered his head, embarrassed. Admittedly, he had forgotten. "Right."

"Speaking of, I got good news, Brie." Brie perked up. "I got word from the Hunter Agency. They accepted the indemnification application. So we're good."

"Indemnifi-Indemni-Indemn... What is this fication?" Ogenos crackled, slightly annoyed.

Steve chuckled. "Whenever a tyrant attacks a business, the Hunter Agency has these forms for the owner to fill out. It's a complicated process, but basically, if they accept it, they compensate the business for the damages caused by the tyrant." He elaborated, though Ogenos was already disinterested. "Usually, that's only for if the building gets destroyed 'cause of fighting between a hunter and tyrant. But we lucked out, so they'll be doing the repairs *and* we'll be getting paid for any days we miss."

"Lucky you."

"Yeah, I guess I am lucky. Good thing, too, 'cause after everything that's happened, I wanna stay home and do a whole lotta nothin.'"

"I guess that gives me time to move in," Brie commented.

"See! Everyone wins."

Ogenos clicked absentmindedly. "Well, if that's it, I'll be going back to the basement now." Steve lazily waved his hand in acknowledgment.

Before he could leave, Val stopped him. "Sir Overlord, what am I to do in the meantime?"

"Shouldn't you be monitoring the empire?"

"I could, but it wouldn't be great. Our transmitters get spotty when they're spread out between dimensions, as expected. Besides, Bellows is handling everything on our behalf."

Ogenos looked over at a nearby book, which was an encyclopedia he had read regarding tyrants. "If you want something to do, then read this." He handed the book to Val, who looked at it with hesitation.

"Sir Overlord, surely you jest?"

"Do I look like a jester to you?"

"I-I meant no disrespect. It's just that, as primitive as this civilization is, it'll take me a few weeks to translate their language. Verbal communication is one thing, but written language takes time."

Ogenos paused. "You can't read their language?"

Val shook his head shamefully. "It is regretful, but I am not as quick as you to decipher such gibberish."

Ogenos had always found it weird how he instantly understood the language employed on Tyran, despite never researching it. He figured it had something to do with crossing the boundaries between universes, but if Val still needed to study the written word, what was different with him?

Ogenos grumbled, confused. "Well, I had to learn the bare necessities. If you wish to stay here, you must as well."

Val clicked slowly, giving Ogenos a disheartened look. Eventually, he took the book. "Very well."

Thinking their conversation was done, Ogenos turned.

"Oh, by the way, Sir Overlord, how did you get here?"

"What?" He turned back to Val.

"You said you transported yourself here to Tyran, did you not?"

"That's correct..."

"Apologies if the question sounds foolish. I'm just confused about how you did it."

"Simple. I used the transporter."

"That's the thing—you shouldn't have been able to." Ogenos tilted his head, which Val took as a sign to continue. "When I showed you the transporter, it was very much still a prototype. Actually, it was more of a work in progress of a prototype."

"But you used it to find me, right?"

"Yes, but only after completing the prototype and syncing it to the mothership's systems. After which, we reused the coordinates that were already inputted on the transporter."

"I don't recall putting in any coordinates. All I did was mess around with the symbols. The next thing I knew, I was here."

"Odd... sounds like it malfunctioned. But even then, it should've only been able to throw you somewhere within our universe."

So, not only was Ogenos able to bypass Tyran's language barrier, but he also should've never made it that far in the first place.

The situation was quite a conundrum. "That is quite the mystery. But unfortunately, other matters call to me." As much as the oddity confused Ogenos, he didn't want to bother with it at this very moment.

Val bowed. "Of course, Sir Overlord. Do not allow me to take up any more of your precious time."

Ogenos returned to his dwelling, the basement. Something about it felt more comfortable than any other room in Steve's house. However, he wasn't here solely for the welcoming atmosphere.

He approached the blade left behind by Platinum, having left it on the round wooden table.

While it was unfortunate the Platinum Brothers died from their encounter, Platinum's blade served as a reminder to Ogenos that he was capable of change. After all, they were the first opponents in his life that he refrained from harming. Not because he had to, but because he wanted to.

Ogenos raised the platinum sword, allowing the jewels embedded within to glimmer in a beautiful display underneath the ceiling light.

He angled the blade, seeing himself in its reflection. "Hmph." He chuckled, hardly recognizing the tyrant that once was.

To think he once thought he needed a clean slate to get what he sought. In reality, all he needed was a fresh start. And now he had it.

EPILOGUE. THE HUNTER AGENCY

"You wanted to see me, Director?" A woman's voice echoed through the quiet room as she stepped inside, her heels clicking and clacking in the darkness.

"Miss Sinclair," the Director addressed, standing at the other end of the room. In front of him was a humongous monitor mounted to the wall, it being the only source of light. "I take it you've heard the news?"

How could she not? It's all the upper echelons of the Hunter Agency talked about.

Platinum and Silver, the only other apex hunters ranked below her. When the agency confirmed their vitals had flat-lined, a terrible pit formed in her stomach. Their deaths herald a bad omen.

Sinclair frowned. "Yeah, I heard. I assume that's why you called me?" She guessed, though if that were the case, it didn't make sense that the Director only called her.

The Director nodded, folding his arms behind his back. "I wanted to show you something."

Sinclair stopped a few feet away from the Director, silently watching him stare up at the large monitor. On the monitor were various smaller screens, each one showing a different location of Valentina City.

One of the screens increased in size, showing a garbled, distorted video. "What is this?"

"Footage. From the other side."

Sinclair raised a confused brow. *"Alright...?"*

"We've deduced the rifts that were appearing around Valentina City were caused by an A-Tier tyrant. We expected this due to the recent attacks. The footage you are seeing now is what our drones were able to capture upon entering one of the rifts."

Sinclair squinted up at the screen. She quickly noticed the footage wasn't video, but rather a bunch of distorted images heavily edited and stitched together.

As the spliced images played, humanoid figures appeared. They looked similar to the insectoids that lived in sprawling colonies underground, though the differences between them were night and day.

"So, the tyrant that killed Silver and Platinum was underground?"

"No. I have reason to believe the culprit was an extraterrestrial tyrant."

Sinclair tore her eyes away from the screen, now beaming at the Director. "Extraterrestrial? You're not suggesting we're dealing with aliens, are you?"

"I am. If my theory holds true, that is."

"What do you mean *if?*"

"The drones we sent were unable to do a thorough investigation on the creatures they encountered, as they became inert after a few minutes. The reason, we assume, was because of range."

"Range?" Sinclair said, breathless. "But all our systems are global."

"I know."

As ridiculous as it all sounded, the Director was never one to lie. Sure, he didn't always tell the full truth. But he never lied.

So, if range was the issue, that could only mean one thing: Wherever the rifts led, they weren't anywhere on Tyran...

"A-Alright, Director. I think I'm hearin' you right. And in the unfortunate chance I am, I gotta ask: what on Tyran were y'all thinkin' when you sent the Platinum Brothers?!" she yelled, being so agitated that her southern accent came out.

As far as she was concerned, this whole operation was performed in the worst way possible. The existence of aliens was one thing. But for the Hunter Agency to engage them when they were so ill-equipped information-wise? It didn't make sense.

When situations like this came up, all apex hunters were briefed and involved immediately. So why—"They insisted." The Director stated, interrupting Sinclair's rambling thoughts.

She paused before biting her bottom lip. *What were those elves thinking?!*

"The brothers perceived the appearance of these rifts to be a warning of some kind. They wanted to deal with the problem as quickly as possible. Even if it meant going in alone."

Everyone knew the Platinum Brothers, as well as their whole family, were psychic to some extent. They couldn't predict the future or use telepathic abilities, but their gut instincts were almost always right.

"Naturally, we sent them in well-prepared. We made sure they took video recorders and transmitters, too. Unfortunately, as I expected, the recorders failed within the first minute of their expedition. As for the transmitters, we only got clear audio when one of them spoke to us. Most of the time, it was just static."

Sinclair still wasn't one hundred percent convinced the Director had done all he could in the situation. She wouldn't bother pressing on the matter further, as in the end, it was for naught.

"As always, the brothers' intuition was correct. The last

transmission I received was of Silver claiming they found the source of the rifts, as well as a tyrant guarding it. Approximately twenty-five minutes later, both of their vitals flatlined at the exact same time."

"That's..." Sinclair was at a loss for words.

To kill two apex hunters at once was already a monumental task. But to kill ones as agile as the Platinum Brothers? Unheard of. The tyrant would've had to have been an S-Tier.

"But the rifts are closed now, so their deaths weren't in vain," Sinclair exclaimed, looking for some hope in the situation.

"I would like to agree. But that is exactly why I called you here." Before Sinclair could question anything, three screens enlarged on the monitor.

The first screen displayed a video feed of Valentine Mall's interior. It looked just as pristine as the articles said, indicating the footage was taken before that B-Tier crabor tyrant attacked.

Suddenly, the lights in the mall repeatedly flashed red, and the crowd scattered in a panic. There was no audio, but Sinclair could imagine the screams of the frightened people.

Eventually, the crabor tyrant busted through the mall's floor. By then, everyone except two people had evacuated. One was a large purple insectoid tailored in hunter-like armor; the other was a regular human dude.

Sinclair watched intently, expecting an unfortunate scene to play out, only to get the shock of her life when the purple insectoid defeated the tyrant in a single move.

She remembered reading the report about a B-Tier tyrant appearing in Valentine Mall—the highlight being the tyrant had already perished by the time hunters arrived at the scene.

It was a big mystery to both the public and agency officials. But now that Sinclair was watching the footage, she wondered how nobody in the agency knew about this. Could the Director be covering it up? If so, why?

As Sinclair's thoughts stewed, the second screen snatched her attention. It was of the same purple insectoid, only this time they were out in Valentina City. There were no flashing red lights this time, but the crowd suddenly panicked, signaling an incoming tyrant attack.

As the people scrambled over one another to escape, a small reptilian girl got separated from her mother. In that brief instance, the crowd swept away the mother.

Meanwhile, the purple insectoid didn't look to be in a hurry. In fact, they ended up protecting the child from the E-Tier tyrants that appeared.

Sinclair was noticing a reoccurring pattern. However, she wondered why the automated defenses for either location failed to start up.

She shook her head and focused on the third screen, which seemed to be the inside of a burger joint. As expected, the purple insectoid was the center of attention, and once again, tyrants appeared. They tore the place up, but thanks to the insectoid and a few of the employees, no one was seriously injured. Sinclair sighed in relief.

"Have you noticed anything?" The Director asked.

"Yeah, two things. The defenses aren't activating, and that purple dude is an unregistered hunter."

"Unregistered hunter, or..." Two screens enlarged. On the right was the purple insectoid, while the left showed the garbled footage of the aliens.

It didn't take Sinclair long at all to piece together both were of the same species, though she mentally slapped herself for not noticing right away.

As if sensing her realization, the Director continued. "The footage you see on the right was captured days before the footage on the left. Considering the close time frame, we believe this individual on the right belongs to the group on the left. For the time being, have decided to call them offworlders."

The right screen enlarged. "This offworlder, in particular, negatively affects our automated defenses whenever they're around. On top of that, they seem to attract tyrants to their location. A terrible combination."

As much as Sinclair wanted to doubt the Director's claims, that'd be the only way to explain all the weirdness going on in Valentina City. More importantly, this revelation cleared up some foggy details regarding the Platinum Brothers' demise.

Still, there was one thing that didn't add up. The offworlders were clearly hostile, considering what they did to Silver and Platinum. However, this purple offworlder was protecting people. Could it be a runaway?

"I don't think this purple offworlder is with the ones that killed Silver and Platinum. If it were, they'd be killing people left and right, wouldn't they?"

The Director shook their head. "I am unsure. However, I am certain that all of these events mean one thing."

Finally, he turned around, now facing Sinclair. The light from the large monitor illuminated their surroundings, including the Director's figure, but his whole front remained shrouded in darkness. The only thing Sinclair could make out were his glowing brown eyes.

"The prophecy."

Sinclair shuddered. "Director, be serious."

"If I weren't, you wouldn't be here." Sinclair's mouth went agape as she finally realized something.

If the prophecy was involved, then there was no wonder why he called her specifically. Assuming it was true, the only person in all of Tyran who could even hope to stand a chance would be the number one apex hunter, Madeline. Her sister.

Now, the Director's actions made sense. Lying to the public about the Platinum Brothers, not calling the other apex hunters, refraining from distributing Valentine Mall's footage to the rest of the agency—he was trying to keep everything under wraps.

"With all that said, this is where you come in." The Director pointed up at the monitor.

Sinclair looked, seeing an enlarged profile of a human man. She recognized him as the same guy who was in the mall alongside the purple offworlder. Come to think of it, he was also in the burger joint.

"Steve Gale." She read his name, looking back at the Director. "What about him?"

"This man seems to be in the good graces of this offworlder. Whether or not he knows as much as we do is currently unknown. Regardless, he is living proof that these offworlders, at least the purple one, are capable of communication and coexistence. He may be our only gateway to discovering who these offworlders are and why they've come."

Sinclair looked at the screen, then back at the Director. "So what? You want me to get on this guy's good side to collect intel on the offworlder?" The Director nodded. "Won't that be a bit too obvious? I mean, it's not every day you see an apex hunter suddenly being all buddy-buddy with a fast-food manager..."

"It won't be as long as we're subtle about it."

"And how exactly am I supposed to be subtle about it?"

The Director stared at Sinclair instead of answering her question. After his dramatic pause, he blinked, followed by the monitor turning off.

The room fell into darkness, leaving only his glowing eyes visible. "I have a few ideas."